As her lips had opened to pronounce his name, he had captured them with his own, his mouth savoring the delicious sweetness of her as he had longed to do since that first morning he'd seen her. He felt her hands move to his shoulders, then creep about his neck as his own hands tightened around her.

He deepened the kiss for an all too brief moment, then lifted his head. Her eyes were closed, the long lashes lying sweetly against her face. He released her slightly, then waited until she gazed up at him. Her expression was one of wonderment and yearning, and a thrill of exaltation shot through him. If he were a few years younger, he would have scaled the stone walls of Windward and shouted his jubilation from the roof. . . .

ROMANCE

By Jeanne Carmichael
Published by Fawcett Books:

LORD OF THE MANOR
LADY SCOUNDREL
A BREATH OF SCANDAL
FOREVER YOURS
MISS SPENCER'S DILEMMA

MISS SPENCER'S DILEMMA

Jeanne Carmichael

FAWCETT CREST • NEW YORK

A Fawcett Crest Book
Published by Ballantine Books
Copyright © 1996 by Carol Quinto

http://www.randomhouse.com

Library of Congress Catalog Card Number: 96-96373

ISBN 0-449-22466-X

Manufactured in the United States of America

First Edition: October 1996

10 9 8 7 6 5 4 3 2 1

Dedicated to a very special young lady,
Tiffany Marie Jenau,
who made her debut to Society
at 8:12 P.M., October 16, 1995

MISS SPENCER'S DILEMMA

Prologue

Lucian, from the height of his imposing thronelike chair, glared at the man standing before him. This thickset provincial, who looked as though he could not detect a fox in a henhouse, was supposed to be the best Bow Street had to offer. He was half tempted to send the fellow away, but he doubted the Magistrate's Court would send anyone else. They'd refused to assign an agent fulltime, and he'd been forced to employ former runners, or runners on leave, himself. Four of them in the last two years, and except for that one instance, they'd not found a trace of the girl.

He sighed, then poured a glass of bootleg brandy from the crystal decanter that stood on the lavish desk. He swirled it in the glass, watching as the late-afternoon sun glinted off the heavy gold signet ring he wore. The man before him shuffled his feet and watched nervously.

After a moment, Lucian slid open a drawer and removed a small gold locket. He hesitated, then pushed it across the vast mahogany desk. Inside were two miniature portraits. "This is the girl. I doubt she has changed much."

Snelling picked up the locket gingerly, then held it up so he could study it in the light from the window. She was a pretty girl, obviously a lady. She didn't look like a thief, but he knew appearances could be deceiving. "How old was she when this was painted?"

1

"She had just turned twenty."

"And the gentleman?" Snelling asked, studying the other miniature in the tiny locket.

"Her brother, but you need not be concerned about him. She is the one I want you to find. I can tell you that she is not staying with any of her friends or acquaintances and she took very little with her, so I suspect she has sought employment somewhere."

"She might have sold the necklace," Snelling suggested, taking another gander at the drawing on the desk. Three dozen diamonds, all of a good size, set in an elaborate gold filigree collar. "The thing must be worth a bloody fortune."

"She did not sell it," Lucian insisted, his light blue eyes as cold as the Thames in December. "The Sunderland Diamonds are priceless, and not a jeweler would risk it. Besides, I know her. The necklace has been in the family for generations. She would starve before she would sell it. No, she is employed somewhere, and I want you to find her."

Snelling nodded. He wouldn't waste breath arguing with this blue-blooded swell, but if the girl *had* sold the diamonds, she could live in comfort for a long time. And there weren't many that would hold on to a family heirloom when it meant starving. Sentiment was nice, but in his experience it didn't count for much when one's belly was growling.

Aloud he said, "You're certain she's still in England?"

"I believe so. There have been reports, glimpses of her. Two years ago, a runner traced her to Shrewsbury. She was employed as a governess, but unfortunately he must have tipped his hand. By the time I arrived, she had disappeared."

"Why didn't he arrest her?"

"For the same reason that you will not," Lucian replied, reaching across the desk to retrieve the locket.

2

He stared at the miniature for a moment, hating the sight of the girl, hating that she had dared to spurn him. But she would pay. He snapped the locket closed and told the runner, "I wish the matter handled discreetly. You are not to approach her in any manner or even speak to her. I do not want her alarmed. Should you find her, you are to send word to me at once and then watch her until I arrive. Is that understood?"

Snelling nodded, his manner servile, but he suspected there was more to this affair than what the swell before him wanted him to know.

"What are you waiting for, then?" Lucian demanded. "I am not paying you to waste time. I shall expect a written report at the end of each month, and I warn you that if you do not exert every effort to find her, I shall know, and you will not receive so much as a penny. Now, if there is nothing else?"

"Uh, they said in Town as 'ow there was a reward if we succeed . . . a hundred pounds, they said."

"The offer of a reward still stands," Lucian said, a strange smile curling about his thin lips. "For either recovery of the diamonds or finding the girl. But don't think to fob me off with a false report. You receive nothing if she disappears before I arrive."

Snelling agreed and backed from the room. When the runner was gone, Lucian rose to his feet. A slender man, he habitually dressed in black. He liked the contrast between his blond hair and pale coloring, and he rather thought the black made him look more powerful. He craved power and wanted those about him to fear and respect him. It had taken time, but now no one dared to gainsay him.

He stepped down from the platform he'd had especially built behind his desk. It gave the illusion that he was taller and allowed him to look down on those who came before him. He crossed to the casement windows that overlooked the sweep of lawn leading down to the cove. Usually the sight soothed him, and he found satisfaction in knowing that everything as far as the eye could see belonged to him.

But not today. He clutched the locket in his fist. Breathing deeply, he slowly opened his long, tapering fingers. She still had the power to infuriate him. He had offered her everything . . . and she, penniless, totally dependent upon him, had not only refused him but run away. They still talked about her in the village, and he knew that some of the men had dared to laugh at him— because of her. But he would put a stop to that. He would find her if it cost him every penny he possessed.

Lucian opened the locket and gazed down at her. Her eyes mocked him. He could almost see her chin lifting in that proud, aristocratic manner she had. Well, she wouldn't look so proud when Bow Street arrested her. . . .

He intended to be there, a witness to her disgrace. He imagined the scene, a cruel smile on his lips. He would laugh when she begged for his help.

Chapter 1

Damaris Montague stamped her tiny foot in frustration. Her green eyes filling with tears, she glared at her aunt, "You want me to be unhappy! No one considers my feelings. No one cares if I am made miserable—"

"Now, Damaris, darling," the widow Throckmorton coaxed, "you will make yourself ill crying like that, and how can you say we do not care when you must know how very fond we all are of you? Why, you are like my own dear daughter."

"If Melody wanted to meet the earl, you would invite him to the ball," Damaris insisted, a catch in her voice.

Her cousin Oliver glanced at her in disgust. "Put a bridle on it, for heaven's sake. Even if I were impertinent enough to call on Lord Dysart, which I assure you I am not, he'd likely set me down as an encroaching mushroom and wish to have nothing to do with us. Is that what you desire?"

Damaris blinked, allowing a huge tear to roll forlornly down her delicate pink and white cheek. Her full lower lip seemed to tremble. "I think it would be only neighborly if you called on him. How can that be thought encroaching?"

"Well, it is, which shows how much you know, and I won't do it," Oliver replied and rose from the breakfast table. "I am going for a ride if anyone wishes to join me. Melody?"

His pretty, dark-haired sister withdrew her fascinated gaze from Damaris, who had perfected the ability to cry without at all marring the beauty of her features. When Melody cried, her eyes and her nose turned red and her skin looked splotchy. Still bemused, she smiled up at her brother. "Thank you, but no. Miss Spencer and I are driving into the village this morning."

Damaris swung around, her pale blond hair rippling in waves down her shoulders, her eyes narrowing. "Are you, indeed? No one bothered to consult me, and must I remind you that Miss Spencer is *my* companion? I suppose it does not occur to you that I might wish her company?"

Juliana Spencer sighed as she glanced around the charming breakfast room at Blandings, where every luxury money could command had been provided. She knew it was time she intervened, but a throbbing headache behind her eyes made it difficult to summon the energy necessary to deal with her charge. There were days, and this promised to be one of them, when she would have gladly resigned her position.

She listened for another moment as Melody apologized, then she interrupted. In the quiet, genteel voice that Mrs. Throckmorton so much admired, Juliana remarked calmly, "Damaris, my dear, if you continue in this vein, you will ruin your looks."

Her charge appeared startled. The tears stopped instantly and she glanced at her companion curiously. "What do you mean?"

Juliana added cream to her coffee and spoke nonchalantly, as though the matter were of little importance. "Why, only that when you frown in that manner, it mars the smoothness of your brow and adds small lines to the corners of your mouth. Of course, every lady must expect to lose some of her looks with the natural passage of time, but I should hate to see your face wrinkled before you are even twenty."

Damaris, at sixteen, could not conceive that she would ever be twenty, much less old and wrinkled. She raised a tentative hand to her cheek and touched the soft skin next to her mouth. "What nonsense," she scoffed, but she flounced out of the room a moment later.

Juliana, knowing Damaris would go directly to her bedchamber and study her reflection in the looking glass, felt a moment's remorse. She knew it was wrong to use Damaris's vanity against the girl, but nothing else seemed to work.

Juliana saw Oliver grin as he followed his cousin from the room, and a moment later she heard him teasing Damaris as he caught up with her in the hall.

"I think Miss Spencer is right. I do believe I see the beginnings of a wrinkle—ow! Why, you little beast. If I get my hands on you, I shall teach you not to throw books at my head—though that is doubtless the only use you have for them."

Melody laughed and begged to be excused as well. "Someone must protect Oliver. Damaris will wring his neck for that ill-judged remark!"

The widow looked after the trio regretfully. "I suppose one must make allowances for Damaris . . . the dear girl had no proper guidance until she came to live here, and for that I shall never forgive Edward Montague. If he had allowed her to come to me as a child, which is what I know her father must have wished, I would have seen to it that she was properly reared. I am sure that nowhere is there a more prettily behaved young lady than my own daughter."

Juliana readily agreed, but she suspected that Melody's exquisite manners were due more to association with the family at the vicarage and to all the books she read than to her mother's influence. The widow was a daughter of a wealthy merchant, and although she possessed the kindest heart imaginable, she lacked that innate sense of decorum that marked a true lady.

Unaware of Juliana's perusal, Mrs. Throckmorton continued, "Edward was so anxious to get his hands on her fortune, he let her do just as she pleased—at least until she ran off with the music master. Lord, Miss Spencer, it was a blessing you happened upon her in that inn. One shudders to think what may have happened otherwise."

Juliana only half listened, for she had heard Mrs. Throckmorton say the same thing, or a variation of it, dozens of times. The lament was always the same. Edward Montague had wanted Damaris to live with him for the same reasons the widow did: both had a son only a few years older than the young heiress—and hopes of keeping her fortune within the family.

Mrs. Throckmorton had welcomed her niece warmly and treated her well. Perhaps too well. She allowed the girl a great deal of freedom and never rang a peal over her head, although Damaris frequently deserved it. The widow was not nearly as tolerant with her own children, scolding them roundly whenever they forgot their manners or foolishly endangered their health. But her lectures sprang from a loving concern and everyone knew it— even Damaris, who was shrewd enough to realize her assorted relatives wanted guardianship of her only because of the fortune she commanded.

Juliana absently brushed a wisp of coppery hair away from her cheek and replied, "It was fortunate for me as well, Mrs. Throckmorton, for I was much in need of a position."

"That may be, Miss Spencer, but there's none that can tell me you couldn't find a better post elsewhere—and have an easier time of it. For all Damaris is my own dear Frederick's cousin, God rest his soul, I would be the first to admit she has been a sad trial. Chasing after this man

8

and that one—," she broke off, shaking her head so that the frizzled blond curls beneath her mobcap seemed to dance.

"She is at the age where gentlemen naturally occupy a great deal of a girl's thoughts," Juliana said. "Have you given any further consideration to bringing her out this year?"

The widow frowned. While she had a high regard for Miss Spencer, they must always disagree on this subject. Aloud she said, "You know I think her too young. There shall be time enough for that next spring."

"I pray you are right, but since Mr. Marling's arrival, it has become increasingly difficult to keep her from behaving improperly. I must tell you, Mrs. Throckmorton, I would not put it above Damaris to try to meet with him secretly. Perhaps, if she knew she was to come out this fall, it would give her thoughts a different direction—"

"Andrew Marling is nothing but a gazetted fortune hunter," the widow interrupted furiously. "I have forbidden Damaris to have anything to do with him. You will not credit it, Miss Spencer, but she wanted me to send him an invitation to our dinner party."

"So she said," Juliana replied, remembering the unpleasant scene in Damaris's bedchamber the previous night. Damaris had thrown a tantrum, ranting that her aunt did not wish her to have any friends and declaring furiously that there was no reason why Marling should not be included among the guests.

Privately, Juliana doubted that there was anyone in all of Chichester who did not know of Damaris's partiality for the young man who'd followed her here from London. Certainly no one within hearing distance of Blandings. She also knew that forbidding Damaris to see Mr. Marling was a futile gesture.

The young girl desperately wanted someone of her own to care about her, a sentiment Juliana could easily

9

understand for she often felt the same. The only difference was that at sixteen she, unlike Damaris, had been the adored and protected daughter of a loving family. And no matter how difficult her life might be at present, she had those memories to sustain her. Damaris had only the knowledge that people catered to her because of her fortune—or her beauty. It made her a troublesome charge and Juliana feared that if Damaris were not allowed some sort of diversion very soon, she would be tempted into running off with Marling or some other gentleman who caught her fancy. However, Mrs. Throckmorton disagreed, and the widow could be as stubborn in her own way as Damaris. Arguing with her would pay no tolls.

Their conversation was interrupted as Melody returned to the room. She looked quite pretty in a sprigged muslin walking dress, with her dark hair brushed to fall in a charming array of curls. In one hand she carried her new straw bonnet, swinging it by its ribbons. With the other, she held open the door for a large English sheepdog who plodded in after her and looked hopefully at the table from beneath the thatch of shaggy white hair that nearly obscured his eyes.

Mrs. Throckmorton frowned. "My dear, I do hope you are not planning on taking that animal into town. I am certain Miss Spencer cannot wish to share a carriage with him."

"Oh, she does not object," Melody assured her mother with sublime, if misguided, faith. "And Faustus can protect us."

From what? Juliana wondered, hiding a smile as she rose. No one with the least pretension to common sense would be intimidated by Faustus. The sheepdog was certainly huge and ungainly, but more likely to lick the hands of any strangers than to scare them off. He also tended to cower under the bed at the first sound of a raised voice.

As Juliana rounded the table, Faustus rubbed against

her skirts, his overgrown body quivering with joy. She stopped to scratch his head just behind the ear and warned him, "You may come with us, but if you dare to romp through one puddle or pond, you shall be made to walk home!"

Left to herself, Juliana would have driven into Chichester in the gig. She was quite capable of handling the reins, and the lack of space would have precluded taking Faustus. Mrs. Throckmorton, however, thought a gig beneath the dignity of the family, and insisted that whenever Miss Spencer had to go into town, she be properly driven in the brougham with Paxton on the box. The widow would have liked to have sent two footmen as well, but there Juliana drew the line.

As it was, she thought the carriage pretentious for someone in her position, but she knew her employer meant it as a kind gesture. And this afternoon she was almost thankful to have Paxton handling the reins. Her headache had increased as the day progressed, and by the time she had fulfilled several commissions for Mrs. Throckmorton, she was tired and suffering from a fit of the blue devils.

The weather only exacerbated her mood, for it had turned chilly and a stiff breeze made it feel even colder. Fortunately the library was their last stop, and as she stepped into the square with Melody, she remarked how pleasant it would be to return home and settle before the fire with a good book and a hot cup of tea.

Melody started to agree, but her words were cut short. They had left Faustus by the carriage with Paxton, but the moment he saw his mistress, he lunged forward. Ripping his leash from the hands of the elderly coachman, the dog bounded across St. Martin's Square. In his enthusiasm, he nearly knocked Melody off her feet.

"Down, Faustus," she commanded as the sheepdog

tried to lick her face. She tried to sound firm, but amusement bubbled beneath the words, and her hands were gentle on his coat, so it was little wonder Faustus ignored her.

Juliana tried to capture the dog's leash, but it was tangled between his paws and her efforts only seemed to excite him. He appeared to think it was some great game they played.

The ribbons to Melody's bonnet came untied, and an instant later the wind picked up the hat and sent it skittering down the square.

"Now see what you've done, you clumsy beast," Juliana scolded.

Melody only grinned. "Watch, Miss Spencer. I've taught him a new trick. Fetch it, Faustus, fetch my hat," she ordered and stepped back. The sheepdog woofed, then lumbered after the bonnet, moving with surprising speed. He captured one of the ribbons as he reached the end of the square, then downed the straw hat with a great paw. After getting a firm grasp on it with his teeth, he turned and started back.

A tall gentleman, about to step into his carriage on the opposite side of the square, paused to watch the chase. As Faustus trotted back with his prize, the man laughed aloud and called out, "Well done, fellow."

Perhaps recognizing the sound of male authority, or merely liking the note of approval in the deep baritone, the sheepdog immediately changed direction. Ignoring Melody's command to return, Faustus dashed across the square and proudly presented his trophy on top of one highly polished Wellington boot.

"Good boy," the gentleman said as he scooped up the bonnet and, at the same time, managed to grasp the dog's leash. "Sit," he ordered firmly, then watched the progress of the two young ladies as they crossed the square.

One was just a girl hardly out of the schoolroom, a

pretty little thing with the promise of beauty to come. He spared her no more than a passing glance and focused his attention on the other miss. He judged her to be about three-and-twenty and uncommonly attractive. As she drew near, he studied the oval face beneath the wide-brimmed bonnet. Blue-green eyes returned his gaze with a composure and gravity belied by the sweet lines of her mouth. She would laugh easily, he thought, then wondered how he knew that.

He studied her, thinking they must have met before. There was something elusively familiar about her, from the color of the deep auburn tendrils framing her face to the graceful arch of brows above the heavily lashed eyes—but the memory escaped him.

"I must apologize, sir," she said, her voice low, musical, with just a hint of the north in it so that it sounded precisely as he had known it would. "I hope the dog did not startle you."

He glanced at the massive bundle of fur panting at his feet. One shiny black eye, visible through the thatch of white hair, looked hopefully up at him, and a pink tongue lolled thirstily. "Hardly the sort of animal to startle anyone, for all he's a clever fellow."

"He truly is," the young girl declared, kneeling to give the dog a hug. "I have just taught Faustus to fetch—only, of course, he was supposed to bring my hat back to me."

"Well, I am very glad he did not," the gentleman responded, presenting her hat with a flourish. "I only wish my own dogs were half as clever. They never fetch anything more exciting than a dead bird."

Melody, suddenly shy of the handsome stranger, ducked her head as she accepted the slightly mangled hat.

Juliana took control of the situation and announced decisively, "We are much obliged to you, sir, but if you will give me his leash, I think we need not trouble you further."

13

"Now, what have I said to make you think you have troubled me?" he asked as he handed over the leash. "If anything, I believe I am indebted to this beast for introducing me to two such charming young ladies."

"A rather unconventional introduction, sir," Juliana replied, and despite her desire not to encourage the gentleman, her lips curved into a smile.

"Perhaps, but . . . I have the feeling we have met before, though the occasion escapes me. I am Valerian Kinborough—"

Surprised, Melody glanced up. "Good heavens—Miss Spencer, it is Lord Dysart!"

He laughed. "In the flesh," he owned, but his gaze returned to Juliana. "Spencer . . . I do not believe I recognize the name."

"And nor should you, sir," Juliana replied, hiding the sudden uneasiness she felt. "It is unlikely our paths would have crossed. I serve as a companion to this young lady, Miss Throckmorton of Blandings, and also to her cousin, Miss Montague."

"Blandings?" he quizzed, ignoring the reference to her position and concentrating instead on her eyes. He knew those eyes. Damn his lamentable memory. Aloud he said, "Why, then, we are neighbors. My estate, Windward, lies just south of Blandings."

"Then undoubtedly we shall meet again. Good day, my lord," Juliana replied with a cool nod of dismissal. To her charge she said, "Come along, Melody. We must not keep your mama waiting."

Dysart watched the lady walk away. She carried herself regally and never once glanced back, not even when she entered the carriage. Miss Throckmorton did, and when she saw him still watching, waved gaily. But not Miss Spencer.

Dysart was not particularly conceited, but he would have to be blind and dumb as a post not to realize that

14

ladies generally found him attractive. They pursued him wherever he went. Of course some of their enthusiasm could be set down to his possession of a title and considerable wealth, but other gentlemen similarly situated were not chased with as much fervor. And rarely had he encountered a lady as unresponsive to his overtures as Miss Spencer.

He smiled, remembering her cool nod of dismissal. Like a duchess, he thought. She might be in reduced circumstances at present, but he would wager his last groat that Miss Spencer came from a well-to-do family and was more accustomed to giving orders than following them. He also suspected he knew her family, or at least some branch of it, for there was a familiarity about her features that tantalized him.

When she had disappeared from view, he stepped into his carriage and met the amused gaze of his secretary, Charles Harrington. "Well?" Dysart demanded. "Have you something to say?"

"No, my lord," the younger man said, but he could not quite suppress a chuckle and in truth did not try very hard. Five years younger than Dysart, Charles had come to him straight out of school, and at first he'd been rather shocked both by his lordship's reputation and conduct. He'd quickly learned, however, that Dysart was not only scrupulously fair but demanded complete honesty from those who served him—even when the truth was not particularly palatable.

Now Charles schooled his features into a look of bland innocence, and added, "I confess I find it rather remarkable the way that dog came directly to you with the young lady's hat."

"Obviously an intelligent animal," his lordship replied with a challenging look. When his secretary merely nodded, he settled back against the cushions and adjusted the lace at his cuffs. "They do say dogs are an excellent judge of character."

"Very true, my lord, but unfortunately it appears the young lady does not share the dog's acumen."

"So it seems, but Miss Spencer does not know me yet," Dysart replied with a smile. "And that, my dear Charles, is a situation I intend to remedy."

Any hopes Juliana had of quietly settling down with a cup of tea and a book were shattered. Melody was unusually animated and though her hat was ruined, she considered it a small price to pay for the pleasure of meeting Lord Dysart—particularly before her cousin had the opportunity to do so. She wasted no time in informing the family of the encounter. Oliver and his mother were as eager as Damaris to learn more about Lord Dysart and plied both Melody and Miss Spencer with questions.

"Is he really as handsome as they claim?" Damaris asked when the details of the meeting had been exhausted.

"More so," Melody replied dreamily. "He is taller than even Oliver and, I think, terribly strong. . . ." She hesitated, then added with a blush, "One could not help noticing his broad shoulders—"

"Are you certain it was not mere padding?" Damaris interrupted.

Melody shook her head. "I think not. He is splendidly proportioned, and even his features have an air of manliness about them. His eyes are dark brown, almost black, and survey one from beneath heavy brows. His face would be harsh were it not for the sweetness of his smile."

"Careful, little cousin," Damaris warned, miffed at the attention Melody was receiving. "Miss Mowbrey said that his smile has seduced more ladies than—"

"Damaris Anne Montague!" Mrs. Throckmorton

scolded. "I will not have such talk in my house, and I will tell you to your head that it is vastly unbecoming for a girl of your age to be speaking in such a manner."

She shrugged. "I am only repeating what Miss Mowbrey said, and she was not the only one. They call him Devil Dysart in Town, you know."

"If that is true, then he is not the sort of person I would wish for either you or Melody to associate with," Mrs. Throckmorton decided—and instantly met with a barrage of protests.

Realizing too late where her boasting had led her, Damaris hastily recanted. "I was merely teasing, Aunt Caroline. 'Tis only idle gossip, I am sure."

"Mama, he was extremely nice and very much the gentleman, was he not, Miss Spencer?"

Appealed to, Juliana hesitated. She did not wish to encourage the family to be on terms with Lord Dysart, but at the same time she knew his reputation was not deserved—at least not entirely. He had been at school with her older brother, and Philip had spoken warmly of Dysart, counting him a good friend. Her sense of fairness prompting her, she finally said, "I think our chance meeting with his lordship was too brief to come to any conclusion. Certainly he conducted himself like a gentleman."

Oliver, who was as anxious to meet Dysart as was his cousin, though he would not admit it, added, "Pay no attention to Damaris, Mama. She hasn't the least notion of what she is saying. Only last week she told me Jeremy Fielding had tried to seduce her, and all he did was write a poem to her eyes."

Damaris looked ready to argue the matter, but Oliver silenced her with a dagger look and continued. "I think, since Melody has met Lord Dysart, we should send him an invitation to the ball tomorrow. He probably will not

17

come, but I should not like to be backward in any attention due him."

Mrs. Throckmorton wavered and the decision might have gone either way, except Melody chose that moment to say ingenuously, "Oh, Mama, only imagine. If he should come, Mrs. Fitzhugh will be green with envy. I will wager she never had an earl attend one of her parties."

The notion appealed. "I suppose it could not hurt to invite him and leave it to Providence whether he chooses to come or not. Melody, dearest, bring me my cards."

Juliana thought it highly unlikely the earl would accept an invitation to a country dinner and ball, especially since he was not acquainted with the host and could not expect to know many of the guests. She said nothing, however, asking instead for leave to be excused.

"Of course, Miss Spencer, of course. There is no need for you to sit here with us, which puts me in mind of something I meant to tell you . . . now, what was it?" She wrinkled her brow in thought, and then suddenly remembered. "Oh, yes. A letter came for you. I had Milly put it in your room."

"Thank you," Juliana murmured, hiding the sudden stab of fear she felt. In the year she had been at Blandings, she had not received so much as one letter. There was no one to write to her, no one who knew where she was residing. Mrs. Throckmorton had once commented on her lack of correspondence, but Juliana explained it away by saying how much she hated writing and that all of her friends knew her to be a poor correspondent. The widow, who did not write many letters herself, had accepted the explanation without question.

But now someone had written her. Uneasy, Juliana stepped into the spacious bedchamber allotted her. She saw the letter at once, propped on the center table next to a vase of fresh flowers. She picked it up gingerly and carried it to the chair near the window.

She noticed at once that the letter was not franked and, without being aware of it, emitted a sigh of relief. Her pulse slowed a little and her heart beat more normally.

Slitting open the envelope, she scanned the nearly illegible lines. The writer was neither educated nor adept at penmanship, though he adopted a flowery style. The lines, crossed and recrossed, were—once she had deciphered them—threatening in their simplicity. A gnawing, hollow feeling rose in her chest as the page trembled in her hands.

Chapter 2

Disbelieving, Juliana read the note again but the words had not changed:

My Dear Miss Spencer,

Although we are as yet unacquainted, I almost feel as though we are old friends. You see I have spent the past six months searching for you at the behest of a gentleman who shall remain nameless, but one whom I believe is well known to you. This gentleman is more than willing, one might even say eager, to pay hand-somely for the knowledge of your whereabouts.

However, inasmuch as I am not kindly disposed toward said gentleman, I might be persuaded to keep such information as I have learned to myself—in re-turn, of course, for suitable payment for the expenses I have incurred. In other words, Miss Spencer, I believe that you and I might come to some arrangement to our mutual benefit.

If you are agreeable, I suggest you arrange for the windows leading to the gardens at the rear of the house to be left unlatched tomorrow evening. At the stroke of midnight, I will then enter the house and we may discuss the details of our little arrangement in privacy. Of course if I find the windows latched, I shall have no choice but to inform our mutual friend of your whereabouts, a course of action that I would under-

take reluctantly, and only from the direst necessity, my
funds being at low tide. You may believe me,
    Your humble servant,
    J. P. Snelling

Angrily, Juliana tore the paper to shreds and then tossed the scraps in the fireplace. The small act of rebellion gave her a moment's sense of satisfaction, but the feeling disappeared as quickly as the smoke from the shards.

During the last few months at Blandings, she had come to believe that Lucian had quit searching for her, that she had found a safe haven. Now her hopes were shattered. Pacing the room, Juliana fought the rising tide of fear that tied her stomach in knots. She forced herself to think clearly. Above all, she must not panic.

She could leave Blandings, disappear tonight as she had twice before when Lucian had discovered her whereabouts. But the thought of running again disheartened her. She recalled all too clearly the humiliation she'd endured traveling by stage, the disdainful looks from innkeepers when they saw she had no maid to accompany her, and the suggestive looks from men who offered her protection of a sort.

Nor had she forgotten the nights she'd gone hungry for fear of using up her meager hoard of savings before she found a position—or the countless ladies who had abruptly terminated an interview when they'd learned she had no references. Fortune had blessed her when she chanced upon Damaris Montague at an inn. The girl had been frightened and near hysterics after discovering that an elopement was not the romantic interlude she'd imagined. Tired and disillusioned, she had wanted only to be rescued.

Juliana had intervened and arranged passage for both of them on the next stagecoach to Chichester, where

Damaris said her aunt resided. The journey had been impossibly long and tedious, for Damaris, once over her initial fright, alternated between bouts of exuberant elation, flirting boldly with the driver and two of the male passengers, and the depths of melancholy at the prospect of residing in the country for the next year. But like Juliana, Damaris had little choice. She had run away from her uncle's home in London and knew he would not have her back again.

However, she was not by any means resigned to her situation. Her aunt, she complained, did not move in the first circles, and likely there would be nothing to do and no one of interest to talk to. Filled with self-pity, Damaris had sulked until Juliana's patience was sorely tried. She had wondered if Mrs. Throckmorton would be quite as pleased to welcome Damaris as the girl claimed. But when they arrived at Blandings, the widow had been overjoyed to receive them both and embarrassingly grateful to Juliana, who she apparently believed was the only person in the world capable of exerting any influence over her wayward niece.

As if conjured up by Juliana's thoughts, Damaris tapped on the door and, without waiting for leave, strolled in. "Someone should have a word with Melody. To hear her talk, one would think she was the only person to ever meet a titled gentleman. I do hope she does not intend to lord it over us at dinner."

Hiding her frustration at the intrusion, Juliana made an effort to appear unconcerned and replied, "I am sure she will not. Melody has excellent manners."

"Oh, pray spare me the lecture. I am weary of hearing how perfect dear little Melody is," Damaris said as she drifted round the room, her sharp eyes taking in every detail. She fingered the ivory-handled brush on the vanity table, examined a book and then laid it down again. She idly picked up the envelope from the center table, while with near-perfect mimicry parroting, "Melody has excellent manners, Melody has a charming disposition, Melody always conducts herself like a lady—honestly, Miss Spencer, do you not think it a trifle odd for anyone to be so well-behaved?"

"No, I do not," Juliana replied as she crossed the room and snatched the envelope out of the girl's hands. "Your cousin has learned the rudiments of polite behavior and you would do well to follow her example. For instance, she would never attempt to read another person's letters."

"Gracious, do not get into a pother. I was merely curious," Damaris said with a laugh and strolled toward the looking glass. She brushed a curl away from her brow while carefully observing her companion's reflection. "You never receive anything in the post. Who is this mysterious letter from? A secret admirer or perhaps someone out of your lurid past?"

"Hardly, since I do not have a lurid past," Juliana replied and busied herself hanging up her pelisse.

"No, you haven't any at all, and I think that very strange."

Juliana turned to face her charge with a mock show of surprise. "I had not realized you were so interested in my history, Damaris, but I own myself much encouraged. Concern for someone else is a sign of maturity I had not hoped to see in you so soon and must be rewarded. Therefore, I will answer any questions you choose to ask. What should you like to know? I was born in a small village north of—"

"Oh, botheration. Forget I asked," Damaris muttered, stomping toward the door. She met Melody just coming in and snapped, "If it isn't little Miss Perfection, still aflutter over meeting her first peer. I warn you I am heartily sick of hearing about it and shall be violently ill if you mention Lord Dysart one more time!"

Melody stared after her cousin for a minute, then stepped into Juliana's room. "What in heaven's name is wrong with Damaris?"

"Pay her no heed. She is only a little jealous of you."

Melody looked her astonishment. "Damaris jealous? Oh, Miss Spencer, surely you must be mistaken. Why, she is so beautiful, she has every gentleman in the county at her feet. You have seen the way they all compete for her attention."

"Not all of them," Juliana said with a smile. "I seem to recall that at the last assembly, you danced just as often as your cousin."

A pair of dimples showed as Melody smiled ruefully. "I did, but half the young men who asked me to stand up did so only because they wished to talk about Damaris."

"Then I suggest you concentrate on the other half," Juliana said, trying to be patient but desperately wishing for a few moments of privacy. She gave Melody a hug, then gently urged her to the door.

"Oh, I nearly forgot. Mama sent me up to remind you that we are having guests for dinner and she particularly wishes you to join us." Melody made a face. "She invited Mr. and Mrs. Yardly, and Frederick, of course, but they also have a young man visiting—some sort of distant connection—and Mama said to tell you the numbers will be uneven if you do not oblige her by sitting down with us."

"If she wishes it, then certainly. Do thank her for me," Juliana murmured. They spoke for another few moments before she could firmly shut the door. Leaning against it, she rubbed her throbbing head. Heaven help her if the widow did not cease playing matchmaker. She knew her employer meant well, but her kindness unwittingly placed Juliana in an extremely awkward position. She could not, under any circumstances, encourage the gentlemen to whom Mrs. Throckmorton introduced her—not Frederick Yardly or Mr. Chadleigh or dear Mr. Simon.

Nor could she tell them the truth. She wished it might be otherwise, wished that she had never met Lucian, that Papa and Philip were still . . . but wishes were a luxury she could no longer afford. Resolutely she crossed the room and tossed Mr. Snelling's envelope into the fire, watching as the flames caught the edges and curled it inward until nothing remained but ashes. If only Mr. Snelling could be gotten rid of as easily.

Juliana knelt in front of the wardrobe and from the bottom removed a small rosewood box that had once belonged to her mother. For a moment, her fingers caressed the intricately worked top. Then she opened it and sighed as she glanced at the pitifully small stack of notes. As she counted them out, she knew it would never be enough to satisfy Mr. Snelling.

Juliana prayed for guidance before retiring, but the night brought only troubled dreams. Despite all her efforts, and even pinching her cheeks to induce some color, she appeared unusually pale when she went down to breakfast Friday morning. The widow was seated at the head of the table, with her daughter on one side and her niece on the other. Oliver, as was his custom, had risen early and ridden out with the estate manager.

Juliana stepped over Faustus, sprawled between her chair and Melody's, and apologized for her tardiness as she took her seat. Mrs. Throckmorton waved her explanations aside. She was too preoccupied with details of the ball that evening to notice how tired Juliana looked, but Melody did and expressed the hope that Miss Spencer was not falling ill.

"Good heavens. She cannot possibly," Mrs. Throckmorton cried, alarmed at the very idea. She turned to Juliana impatiently. "Why, we shall have a house full of guests this evening. I could not possibly manage without your assistance."

Juliana knew her employer was not as coldhearted as she sounded. Mrs. Throckmorton always agonized over giving a party and, despite numerous successes, remained fearful that something dreadful would go wrong. Hoping to reassure the older woman, Juliana determinedly set her own problems aside and forced a smile to her lips. "Pray, do not worry, ma'am. I shall be better directly. 'Tis only that I did not sleep well."

"I wonder why," Damaris said, gazing at her companion with a show of bland innocence. "Oh, dear, I do hope the letter you received did not contain bad news?"

"How kind of you to be concerned," Juliana replied while suppressing a strong urge to strangle her charge. But there were other ways of dealing with her, and she neatly turned the tables by remarking, "Speaking of letters, have you answered your uncle's? It must be nearly a month since he wrote."

Appalled, Mrs. Throckmorton turned to her niece. "A month! Good heavens, Damaris, you must write to him at once. Edward will think it is my doing that you have not done so, and before you know it, we shall have him posting down here."

"I planned to write Grandmama this morning," Melody told her cousin. "If you like, we could do our letters together."

Damaris shook her head. "Thank you, but unfortunately I promised Cressy Milhouse I would call today, and you know what Miss Spencer says about keeping one's promises."

"And I thought you never heeded my precepts," Juliana said, while wondering how anyone who appeared so angelic could be so provoking. Eyeing her charge suspiciously, she added, "I shall, of course, go with you."

"Pray do not trouble yourself. 'Tis only Cressy's after

all, and you would be bored beyond bearing," Damaris protested, barely masking her dismay. "Besides, with the party tonight, I am sure Aunt Caroline will have need of you here. Melody can come with me."

"Melody may indeed come with us, but I would be most remiss in my duties if I allowed either of you to go unchaperoned. As for the party, I am certain that if there is aught left to do, I can tend to it when we return—while you write to your uncle."

Damaris subsided, but it was clear she was not happy. When she and Melody left the room a few moments later, Caroline Throckmorton sighed. "Such a difficult child, but truly, Miss Spencer, if you do not wish to accompany her, I am sure there can be no need. I do not expect you to spend every moment of your time with Damaris."

Juliana nodded to the footman to refill her coffee cup, then waited till he withdrew before confiding, "Perhaps I am wrong, but I suspect Damaris may have persuaded Miss Milhouse to invite Andrew Marling to call this morning."

"Oh, surely not?" the widow protested, but shades of doubt clouded her eyes, and in another moment she was convinced that such must be the truth. "I suppose that would account for Damaris's being so anxious to visit— and it was apparent she did not wish to have your company. Of course that settles it. You must go with her—I do hope you are feeling well enough?"

Juliana nodded as she heard the girls returning and rose reluctantly—nearly tripping over the sheepdog. Sensing an outing, the animal had lumbered to his feet and stood eagerly wagging his tail.

. Melody glanced at him and appealed to Juliana, "Miss Spencer, do you not think we could take Faustus? He could stay in the—"

"I will not sit in the carriage with that creature,"

27

Damaris warned. "You may wish to arrive at Miss Milhouse's with dog hair all over your dress, but I do not."

Juliana sided with Damaris, convincing Melody that it would be unfair both to Paxton and to Faustus to take the sheepdog along. Melody agreed reluctantly, but had to console the dog with half a scone and several slices of bacon before she could be persuaded to fetch her bonnet and gloves. Damaris tapped her foot impatiently all the while, but despite the delay, it was not quite noon when the trio set off.

"Are you certain Miss Milhouse is expecting a call so early?" Juliana asked, once settled in the carriage.

Damaris nodded sulkily. "I told her it would have to be early, because of the ball this evening. She has probably been on the watch for me this last hour."

"Obliging of her," Juliana commented dryly. "Tell me, who else will be present this morning?"

Damaris glanced at the window with studied indifference. "I am sure I could not say. Cressy mentioned something about possibly inviting a few other friends."

Juliana would have questioned her further, but she caught sight of three riders approaching on the other side of the carriage. She immediately recognized Oliver on his large gray horse as well as one of his companions, mounted astride a handsome chestnut.

Melody, too, had spied the riders. With a squeal, she demanded Paxton stop the carriage, then babbled excitedly, "It is Oliver—and he has Lord Dysart with him! Oh, Paxton, do pull up."

As their old coachman drew the team to the side of the lane, Juliana watched the trio of horsemen canter down the hill. Oliver always rode well, more at home on a horse than he ever was in a drawing room, but it was Lord Dysart who drew her eye. He rode a showy chestnut with four white stockings—a prime bit of blood, her brother would have said—but it was the man, not the horse, that attracted her attention.

Clad in a dark green riding coat that only emphasized his broad shoulders and buff pantaloons that molded muscular thighs, Dysart looked handsome enough to catch the eye of any young lady. He had a natural air of command. He might handle the reins casually, but there was no doubting he was in control. An air of confidence, of self-assurance emanated from him, as noticeable as the easy smile on his lips.

Oliver greeted his sister carelessly, then introduced Damaris to Lord Dysart and Mr. Harrington, whom he'd met out riding. Damaris simpered and batted her eyes at the earl, clearly expecting him to be as bowled over by her beauty as most young men were. Dysart, however, gave her no more than a polite greeting before grinning at Melody and inquiring after Faustus.

While his lordship was preoccupied, Oliver introduced Charles Harrington to Miss Spencer. The secretary's serious eyes surveyed Juliana curiously, for his employer had referred to her several times during the previous evening. Charles thought her attractive enough, but nothing out of the ordinary, though he owned her manner was flawless and she conducted herself just as she ought. Not like the spoiled but beautiful Miss Montague sulking in the corner of the carriage. He spoke idly to Juliana for a moment or two, then frowned at Damaris, before courteously inquiring if she were suffering from a headache.

Juliana, choking back a gurgle of laughter, glanced quickly away only to encounter Dysart's dark eyes. She drew in her breath sharply, for his gaze raked her with an intensity she'd never before encountered. Black eyes, black as a storm-swept night, held her mesmerized while he seemed to plumb the depths of her soul.

The sound of Oliver's laughter abruptly recalled her to her surroundings, and Juliana hastily lowered her eyes, breaking the spell Lord Dysart had cast. For a moment, just a moment, she'd imagined there was a feeling of kinship between them. Foolish of her, she thought, for she knew his lordship could have no more than a cursory interest in a mere companion. Dangerous, too, to respond so readily to his practiced charm. She could not afford to be on terms with Dysart. Seeking a distraction, her glance fell on his mount and she murmured, "A beautiful animal, my lord."

"Conqueror is a champion," Dysart replied, caressing the animal's silky neck. There was pride in his voice as he told Juliana, "You would not credit it, had you seen him a few years ago. He belonged to this old farmer who neglected him shamefully. When I first laid eyes on Conqueror, his coat was rough, his mane impossibly tangled, and, judging from the way his ribs showed, he'd not had sufficient to eat in a year. A friend who was with me thought I'd windmills in the head when I offered to buy him—but Conqueror has repaid me tenfold. There's not a horse in the county who can touch him."

Conqueror. The name conjured up bittersweet memories. Juliana recalled her brother, sent down from Oxford for some minor indiscretion, telling her about the horse his friend had bought for a song. The animal had looked dead on its feet, just a nag, Philip had said, but his friend, Val, had seen his potential and nourished him back to health. He'd named him Conqueror and the horse had lived up to the name, winning dozens of races at Oxford until word got about and no one would challenge them. Philip had been so excited, so full of life. . . .

"Miss Spencer?"

She looked up and saw only warm sympathy reflected in Dysart's eyes.

"Was it something I said?" he asked, his voice pitched intimately low.

She felt a strong, unreasonable urge to confide in him,

30

to tell him about Philip and what she was doing at Bland-ings, oddly confident that he would understand. It was irrational of her, and she knew it, but she would have given in to the temptation had he not chosen that moment to smile. It was a charming, flirtatious smile—one that had no doubt successfully seduced scores of young ladies.

"A moment ago your eyes held the sunlight and all the glory of a beautiful morning, but now you look as if someone just broke your heart. If there is anything I can do?"

She smiled wryly. "Are you a mender of broken hearts, my lord? Judging from your reputation, I rather thought you to be the cause of them." Her voice mocked him and the words cut just as she'd intended. But when his smile disappeared, she felt a small twinge of regret. Well, what did he expect? She was no green girl to be taken in easily with soft words and pretty compliments.

"I doubt your heart is in any danger, at least not from me," he replied glibly, but he could not quite hide the flare of irritation in his eyes. He backed his horse a pace or two and spoke abruptly to his secretary. "Charles, I think it is time we returned to the house. Ladies, I bid you good day, but I shall look forward to seeing you this evening."

"Oh," Melody cried. "Are you coming to our ball, then? How splendid."

Dysart's eyes softened at her words. "Thank you, Miss Throckmorton, that is kind of you. I hope you will grant me the pleasure of leading you out?"

Shyly, her cheeks suffused by a becoming blush, Melody nodded.

"Until this evening, then," Dysart said. He did not look in Juliana's direction but lifted his riding crop in a jaunty salute before turning his horse and cantering up the hill. His secretary nodded somberly to the ladies, then followed suit.

"He's a great gun," Oliver declared, watching the pair ride off. "Not at all high in the instep—"

"Well, I did not think him anything special," Damaris declared.

"Why? Just because he didn't fall all over his feet paying court to you? You'll catch cold flirting with him. Lord Dysart ain't one of your tame lapdogs, Cousin!"

Ignoring him, Damaris turned pointedly to her companion. "Can we not drive on, Miss Spencer? I am sure Cressy must be wondering what can have delayed us."

"Don't let me keep you," Oliver said. "I've better things to do with my time."

On the crest of the hill, Lord Dysart brought Conqueror to a halt and looked down at the carriage rolling sedately along the lane. He had accepted young Throckmorton's invitation because he'd wanted to see Miss Spencer again. It annoyed him that he could not think of who she reminded him of, and the feeling that he should know her was just as strong this morning as it had been the previous day.

He was convinced by both her bearing and demeanor that she had to be of genteel birth—some lady of good family fallen on hard times or, he thought suddenly, sent to live in this remote part of the country after being disgraced by scandal. That might account for the rebuff she'd given him when he'd tried only to be friendly. Although the lady seemed to have unaccountably taken him in dislike, he would swear she was not indifferent to him. Of course her behavior was understandable if she wished to avoid him because she feared he would recognize her. Racking his brain, Dysart tried to recall recent scandals, and lord knew there were plenty among the ton, but he could think of no lady who would fit Miss Spencer's description.

Beside him, Charles Harrington watched the departing

carriage and speculated on how long they would remain at Windward. His lordship had said a week, a fortnight at most—just long enough to see to some necessary repairs on the estate. But now Charles suspicioned their stay might be extended, a prospect that did not displease him. The trio of ladies from Blandings would make the visit interesting.

"What did you think of her?" Dysart asked, breaking into his thoughts.

Bemused, Charles answered without thinking, "A beauty, my lord, but rather spoiled. She will require a firm hand on the reins."

Dysart stared at him, astonished. "I would not describe Miss Spencer in those terms—"

"My pardon, my lord. I was speaking of the heiress, Miss Montague."

Dysart laughed, the rich tones carrying across the hills. "Forget her, Charles. Even if she weren't above your touch, she's the sort who will lead the gentleman unfortunate enough to catch her in a merry dance. Miss Montague is pure trouble."

"Do you think so, sir? I realize she is rather young and needs guidance, but I would think her character not yet formed. Of course, I am merely speculating. She is, as you say, above my touch."

"Take my advice and turn your attention to Miss Throckmorton. When you get ready to set up house, she is precisely the sort of girl you should consider wedding— well mannered, dutiful, a bit reserved—she would do you admirably."

"I shall bear it in mind," Charles murmured.

"Do," Dysart said, turning his horse. "And I shall try to heed my own advice. Neither of us needs a female who would stir up nothing but trouble."

"Are you referring to Miss Spencer, my lord? I thought

her rather quiet and dignified, not at all the sort to cause a dustup."

"Which shows how little you know about women, Charles. Trust me, in her own way, Miss Spencer could prove much more troubling than the little heiress. I shall put her out of mind," Dysart said firmly, after one last look at the carriage before it disappeared around the curve in the road.

"You must know best, sir," Charles agreed, aware of his employer's considerable experience with ladies. Indeed, it was the one aspect of his present position that troubled him sorely, for he had been raised to believe that ladies were to be treated with respect and consideration—not bedded as the opportunity arose and then blithely discarded.

He glanced at Dysart, noting the frown that drew his lordship's heavy brows together. It appeared his employer was correct in one regard—Miss Spencer was already troubling him more than any other lady had ever done.

Chapter 3

The ballroom at Blandings overflowed, the guests spilling into the hallways and out onto the balconies for a breath of cool air. Gay chatter and laughter rose above the strains of the small orchestra until the room swelled with sound. Dozens of candles cast their flattering light on the young ladies clad in their finest gowns and the gentlemen dressed in formal attire for the occasion. It was true that the collars of some of the gentlemen had wilted from the excessive warmth of the room, and the coiffures of several ladies fell damply to their brows after their exertions on the dance floor, but no one complained.

Mrs. Throckmorton, from the vantage of her raised seat at the north end of the grand ballroom, surveyed the assemblage with an air of pleased triumph. Juliana, watching her, smiled. If crowding indicated a success, her employer had every right to crow. Although Mrs. Throckmorton had sent out twice the number of invitations she thought necessary to fill the room, on the theory that at least one-third would decline, not a single person had sent regrets. Which, Juliana thought wryly, was probably due to the rapidly spread news that the infamous Lord Dysart would be in attendance. Despite the gentleman's reputation as a hardened bachelor and rake, every mama in the county with a daughter of marriageable age had appeared, seeking an introduction to his lordship.

Juliana spied him across the room, near the tall windows opening onto the south terrace. The moment he stepped off the dance floor, he was surrounded by a bevy of young people. It had been that way all evening. The gentlemen admired his dress and air of sophistication—town bronze, Oliver called it. As for the young ladies, it was easy enough to see why they found Dysart attractive.

Despite the warmth of the room and the crowding, he appeared as cool and as immaculately elegant as when he'd arrived. But there was nothing ostentatious about his attire. If anything, he dressed far more somberly than Juliana would have expected. His dark blue dress coat, though superbly cut to fit snugly over his broad shoulders, possessed neither wide lapels nor ornamental trim. Below it, buff pantaloons molded his muscular limbs down to midcalf, where they snugly buttoned over silk stockings—quite plain by most standards. His waistcoat was brilliantly white, as was the silk cravat tied at his throat, but his collar stood only moderately high and was unadorned save for a discreet gold stickpin.

No one could fault Lord Dysart for his dress or manners, Juliana thought, irrationally annoyed. After their encounter earlier in the day, she had not expected him to pay her much heed, and, at first, he'd been noticeably cool. But as dinner progressed, Dysart seemed to forget their contretemps and plied her with questions about her past. She'd tried several times to turn the conversation, but although his manner was charming, he persisted with the tenacity of a bulldog. His probing questions left her uneasy, and she already had sufficient to worry her.

The thought of her midnight tryst with Snelling brought a frown to her face and an uncomfortable feeling of tightness to her chest. She dreaded the coming confrontation and had fretted over it for most of the day and evening, trying desperately to find a solution to her problems. Nothing had occurred to her except to explain her situation to Snelling and plead for mercy.

Trying to calm her jittery nerves, Juliana reminded herself that the gentleman did not sound as though he were a hardened blackmailer, and in his letter he'd hinted that he did not like Lucian—a statement she could easily believe. Remembering Lucian, she shuddered. He was not the sort of man to inspire any of the warmer emotions. He had no friends that she knew of, and even the servants, who owed him their loyalty and livelihoods, viewed him with contempt. They obeyed him without question—but out of fear, not respect. Juliana could not fault them, for she feared him too much herself. Snelling, however, seemed made of sterner stuff and willing to brave Lucian's wrath. She clung to that one small hope.

Earlier in the day, she had thought it all out, but now, as midnight drew near, her reasoning seemed spurious, and letting a stranger into the house a betrayal of Mrs. Throckmorton's trust. She wished, once again, that there was some other way, but she had not been able to think of anything. She recalled her grandfather's maxim that when something unpleasant had to be done, it was best to get it over with at once. Moving closer to the door, Juliana discreetly observed the time. Only twenty minutes remained until midnight.

She cast one last glance about the room to make certain Damaris was behaving. Twice this evening, Juliana had chased her charge in from the far end of the balcony, where she'd strolled with her escort. The boys involved were both nice lads from respectable families who could be trusted to keep the line, and had they stepped out with any other young lady nothing would have been said. But Damaris had incurred the wrath of several older ladies in the neighborhood and they watched her eagerly, all too ready to fan the fires of gossip.

Bad enough that this morning Damaris had conspired

with Miss Milhouse to arrange a meeting with Andrew Marling. That foppish young man had been on the watch for their carriage and run out eagerly when they'd arrived. The dismay on his face when he saw Juliana had been ludicrous. Although her presence had spoiled their plans to some extent, Juliana had not been able to entirely prevent Damaris from speaking alone with Marling. And what devilment the child planned, Juliana feared to guess.

A flurry of movement signaled the start of the last set, after which the gentlemen would lead the ladies belowstairs to partake of a light buffet. The country dance was designed to end at midnight.

Juliana spotted her charge amid the couples taking their place on the dance floor and breathed easier. Damaris had awarded Michael Allerton, one of the most popular young men in the county, the privilege of standing up with her for this set, which also meant he would be the chosen beau to escort her down to dinner.

Allerton led her out proudly, his grin acknowledging the envious looks of his friends, while Damaris held her head high and looked neither right nor left. She pretended to be oblivious to the admiring glances, but Juliana knew she reveled in the attention, and tonight it was well deserved. Even the sternest critic would have to own that Damaris looked breathtakingly lovely in a simple gown of pale yellow, set off with silver ribbons. The excitement of the evening had added a becoming touch of color to her complexion, and her large green eyes shimmered with the reflected light of the candles.

"She is beautiful," a soft voice murmured in Juliana's ear. "And safely occupied until the end of the set. You may relax your vigilance, Miss Spencer."

Startled, she turned to find Lord Dysart standing close beside her. Ignoring his very inappropriate remarks, she stammered, "I—I rather thought you would be dancing, my lord."

"And so I would be if a certain lady would do me the honor of standing up with me."

Flustered by the teasing look in his eyes, Juliana averted her own gaze and gestured toward the far wall where a number of young ladies strolled about or sat with their chaperons. "I am certain, sir, that you have only to ask."

"I have, but the lady refused me—fobbed me off with some nonsense that as a chaperon she is not permitted to dance."

His voice, pitched low for her ears alone, sent a delightful warmth surging through her veins. Just for a second she thought how wonderful it would be to step out on the floor with him, to return his teasing with the sort of lighthearted banter he so obviously enjoyed. But she was not in a position to do either, and she resolutely ignored the temptation. "You are mistaken, my lord. 'Tis not nonsense but duty that keeps me off the dance floor."

"Ah, but I asked Mrs. Throckmorton's permission and she said that of course you are allowed to dance. Indeed, she said she quite considers you one of the family."

"Mrs. Throckmorton is extremely kind, my lord, but I know my duty even if she does not, and you must see that it would be reprehensible of me to take advantage of her generosity."

He sighed. "You make the performance of one's duty sound an unpleasant burden, Miss Spencer. I cannot help thinking you are acting most unwisely—that is, if you mean by your conduct to set an example for Miss Montague. However, if you are determined on such a course, I shall bear you company."

Thinking she could not have heard him right, Juliana turned. "I beg your pardon?"

His eyes twinkled but he shook his head gravely. "Is it

not obvious? By your example, you are surely teaching Miss Montague that adherence to one's duty means forsaking all pleasure. Hardly an effective measure, I should think, for one of her nature. Only think how much more of an impression it would make were she to observe you dancing with me. Together, we could show her that duty and pleasure may be agreeably intermingled."

"I think not," Juliana said firmly. "The sort of bogus reasoning you suggest has been the downfall of many a young person. I would much prefer for Miss Montague to learn that duty brings its own rewards."

"Indeed?" His right brow rose a quarter inch, and the corner of his mouth quivered. "Pray enlighten me, Miss Spencer. Perhaps you may even incline me to do my duty in the House of Lords, which my secretary has been after me to do this past year or more. What rewards does duty bring?"

"There is satisfaction in knowing one has done as one ought—"

"Unappealing," he interrupted.

"Pride in one's accomplishments," she suggested.

He shook his head. "Boring."

"The good opinion of one's friends and neighbors?"

"They will think what they like regardless."

Juliana shook her head sadly, ignoring the amusement in Dysart's dark eyes. "It is obvious you do not wish to be convinced, my lord, and therefore attempting to persuade you of anything is quite pointless. Pray excuse me."

He restrained her with a hand laid lightly on her arm. Looking down at her, he coaxed, "But you have said little that is persuasive and nothing at all that applies to the instance in question. Do not run away, Miss Spencer. Come dance with me instead."

Exasperated, Juliana stepped away from his touch. "I see that nothing less than frankness will serve, my lord.

40

Very well then. Permit me to say that while my duties as a chaperon may prevent me from dancing, they also save my toes from being trod upon, my nostrils from the odoriferous effect of gentlemen who have overexerted themselves, and my ears from the recitation of hunting exploits that, in some persons, passes for polite conversation. And if you think that does not, in some measure, comprise a reward for doing one's duty, I must take leave to tell you that you are grievously mistaken. Now, my lord, duty dictates that I have a word with the butler before the guests descend for dinner. And if you, sir, have the least pretension to being a well-mannered guest, you will now ask one of the young ladies as yet without a partner to stand up with you."

She was out the door before he could protest further, and when she glanced back she saw him standing where she'd left him, grinning ruefully. Well, at least, she thought as she hurriedly sped down the stairs, he takes a set-down in good form.

She ignored the salon on the lower floor where tables had been set up, and the appetizing aromas from the buffet that wafted into the hall, turning right instead toward the library at the rear of the house.

When she entered, she glanced apprehensively about, but the huge room appeared deserted. The few candles Mrs. Throckmorton had ordered lit, in case a guest wandered down in search of a moment's repose, cast eerie shadows across the Axminster carpet and the glass-fronted cabinets that housed an extensive collection of books. Nervously, Juliana made certain the tall windows leading to the terrace were unlatched. Then she closed her eyes, murmuring a brief prayer.

Dysart spent no more than a moment admiring the fleeing form of Miss Spencer. He could not afford to. Out of the corner of his eye, he saw Mrs. Cavanaugh bearing down on his right, her eldest daughter trailing reluctantly in her wake. The girl was pleasant enough and not entirely unattractive, but she lacked any conversation. When they'd been introduced earlier, she'd answered his few questions with monosyllables, making it clear she wished to be elsewhere. He had no desire to repeat the experience. To his left, he spied Miss Fitzhugh and her friend Miss Chadleigh, their blond heads bent in conversation, giggling loudly as they determinedly approached him. Whether it was well mannered or not, Dysart cravenly darted into the hall and followed in Miss Spencer's footsteps down to the salon.

He found it a spacious room, cleverly decorated with large tubs of red and white carnations from the Throckmortons' greenhouse, the effect doubled by the use of long mirrors hung behind each grouping of plants. The flowers were interspersed with a number of fine oil paintings and the whole lit by four large chandeliers. The color scheme was repeated throughout the room at dozens of small tables, each sporting a gleaming white cloth topped by a small vase of red carnations. The effect was very pretty, but Dysart spared it no more than a glance.

His dark eyes scanned the room. Some of the guests had wandered down with the intention of either securing a table or filling plates from the laden sideboard before the best of the delectable dishes were devoured, but there was no sign of Miss Spencer. He spoke absently to a number of people, received several invitations to join various parties, all of which he politely declined. Mrs. Throckmorton employed an excellent cook, but he'd eaten his fill at dinner. What he wanted now was a smoke.

Turning back toward the hall, Dysart spied young Throckmorton coming in with Charlotte Chadleigh, Miss Trilby, and another young gentleman.

Oliver spotted him at the same moment. "Lord Dysart! Would you care to join us for a bite to eat? We would be pleased to have you."

"Thank you, Throckmorton, and perhaps I shall later, but what I would truly like now is a cigar. Can you show me the way out to the terrace?"

"Certainly, sir." Begging Charlotte Chadleigh's leave, Oliver led Dysart into the hall and pointed out a door standing open. "That's the blue salon, and it opens up onto the gardens. Mama has set candles out, so you shall not have any problem finding your way."

Dysart followed the boy's directions and presently stepped out into the cool night air. He breathed a sigh of relief, grateful for a few moments' quiet. The flagstoned terrace was deserted but he suspected it would not remain so for long. Too inviting to step out in the cool air and take advantage of its dimly lit recesses.

Not wanting company, he lit a cigar and strolled toward the far end of the terrace, his thoughts centered on Miss Spencer. The lady continued to intrigue him. He had arrived at Blandings determined to heed his own advice and put Miss Spencer from his mind. But after listening to the lilt in her voice, which still sounded hauntingly familiar, and observing the grave way she had of tilting her head to one side when she considered a question, he was more convinced than ever that he knew her—or should know her. Even the lighthearted banter they'd shared in the ballroom had only served to increase his certainty. Their conversation had put him strongly in mind of someone, someone with whom he'd been on easy terms. Twice he'd nearly come up with a name—it had been on the tip of his tongue but remained elusively, frustratingly, just out of reach.

A furtive movement from the gardens caught his eye, and he cautiously froze where he stood. As he watched, a tall, shadowy figure emerged from the gardens and entered the house through the tall windows at the corner. The man never hesitated, so it seemed that he was expected. Amused, Dysart wondered if he was witnessing an assignation. Had Miss Montague found a way to see her beau after all? Dysart had heard all about the heiress and her blighted romance with Andrew Marling from young Throckmorton and wouldn't put it beyond the little baggage to arrange a tryst just when most of the guests would be preoccupied with dinner.

He had no desire to spy on the girl or to interfere with her romance, but just on the off chance that he was wrong and mischief might be afoot, Dysart edged closer to the house. He had a clear view of the tall windows leading into the library. Astonished, he drew in a sharp breath. Wrong on both counts.

It was not Miss Montague who nervously greeted the intruder, and it was obviously not a romantic tryst. What the devil was Miss Spencer about?

The man, clad in a heavy greatcoat, had the look of a bruiser or perhaps a coachman down on his luck. When he snatched off his beaver hat, unkempt gray hair sprung out in a riot of curls, matching the untidy beard that covered the lower part of the fellow's face. Even in the dim candlelight, Dysart could see the man's coat was badly stained and his boots had never had the loving care of a valet. Definitely not a gentleman. Miss Spencer, who had backed away from the man, had her hands clasped tightly together—to keep them from shaking? Dysart wondered. She appeared pale, and Dysart had the distinct impression she feared the man.

He crept closer to the windows, concealing himself behind a garden statue of a Greek goddess but ready to interfere if the lady required assistance. From his hiding place, he could just hear threads of the conversation.

"But Lucian is lying," Miss Spencer cried suddenly, and in her agitation, her voice rose, carrying easily to the

44

terrace. "You must see that—he lies about everything. I never took the diamonds. When I left, I carried only my clothes and a few keepsakes from my mother. Even had he offered them to me, I would not have accepted them. I wanted nothing from him!"

Alarmed, the intruder looked around fearfully, then tried to hush her. "Keep your voice down, lady! We don't want the bleeding household in on this business, do we?"

"Oh, what does it matter?" she demanded, plainly distraught. She held out her hands toward him. "Arrest me then, if you think I stole the jewels. Lucian has made these horrible accusations, and I will answer them. Let everyone know the truth about him."

Concerned, Dysart tried to get a clearer view and nearly knocked the statue from its pedestal. It wobbled precariously, but he caught it just in time, replaced it firmly, then peered around it. The man was shaking his head. He kept his voice low and Dysart had to strain to hear the words.

"That's not what he be wanting, miss. I was told just to find you. Why, he would likely have my head if he knew I'd warned you. It's a risk I'm taking, miss, coming to you, but this assignment don't sit right with me. Seems to me he's a lot more interested in finding you than in any diamonds."

"That may be," Miss Spencer replied, sounding somewhat calmer. "But I fear you have wasted your time, Mr. Snelling. I could never pay you what Lucian can. Despite what you may think, I do not have the jewels, nor any income save for the small sum I receive as a companion, and I could not even give you that until next quarter day."

"But all I'm asking is a pittance," the fellow whined. "Just enough to pay my way back north. I'll take your word you don't have the jewels, but what about that bauble on your finger? I'm thinking it would fetch a pretty price."

She covered the small ruby ring with her other hand as though to protect it. "This belonged to my mother, sir. I could not possibly sell it."

The man shrugged. "If I was you, I'd think twice over it, miss. I ain't asking much—just fifty pounds to cover what it cost me to find you—but if you can't pay it, then I'll have to go back and report, and I don't believe you'd be liking that. Tell you what, miss. I'll bide a bit at the inn whilst you think on it. I'll come back in a week for your answer."

"It's useless, sir. I cannot—"

"Don't be hasty, miss. Next Friday," he interrupted, backing toward the terrace. "Same time, same place."

Dysart, hidden behind the statue, held his breath as Snelling took his leave. The man moved easily for one of his bulk, and it was only a moment before his silhouette blended into the deep shadows of the garden, then disappeared. Dysart glanced around. Miss Spencer stood at the windows of the library, staring out into the night.

He waited for her to withdraw, but she remained at the window. He was trapped. If he stepped out now, she would know he'd eavesdropped on her conversation, and he could imagine her embarrassment—and resentment.

He caught the sound of voices emerging into the night at the far end of the terrace and breathed a sigh of relief. In a few more moments, he could casually join the other guests. He stepped back a little to make certain he was in the shadows and nearly tripped. A heavy weight knocked against his knees. Alarmed, he glanced over his shoulder.

Where in the devil had the dog come from? "Go away," he whispered urgently as Faustus butted against him. The sheepdog's tail wagged rapidly, beating a tattoo against the pedestal. To Dysart, the sound seemed omi-

46

nously loud. "Down," he ordered furiously as he saw Miss Spencer glance in his direction.

Faustus half obeyed—the front half. His enormous paws stretched out and his huge head lowered over them, but his rump remained high in the air and the tail wagged as though this were some sort of new game.

Dysart knelt to the dog's level and had his face thoroughly washed by a large, wet tongue. "Stop it, you bloody beast," he hissed, shoving the furry head down.

Mistakenly taking this as some sort of approval, the dog tried to wiggle onto Dysart's knees, panting happily. Giving up the battle, the earl allowed two great paws to rest on his buff pantaloons and brushed the long hair from the animal's eyes. It seemed to quiet the beast, and he gently scratched behind the dog's ears.

Crouched uncomfortably behind the statue, half of the dog's weight on his knees, Dysart silently urged the couples filling the other end of the terrace to stroll in his direction, but they remained obstinately near the doors of the salon.

Just when he thought he could bear it no longer, he heard Miss Throckmorton's voice.

"Faustus, come here, Faustus," she called, searching along the terrace. "Faustus, where are you?"

The sheepdog turned his head in the direction of her voice, then peered up at Dysart, obviously torn. "Pray don't let me keep you," the earl urged, gently pushing the dog off his knees.

At the same instant, Miss Spencer stepped out onto the terrace. "Melody, my dear, I heard you calling Faustus. Surely you did not allow him out among the guests? You know your mother will not approve."

"I'm trying to find him before she finds out," Melody replied, exasperation underscoring her words. "I left him in the kitchen, but Marybell said he was whimpering and she didn't think it would do any harm to let him out in

47

the kitchen garden. Of course he took off like a shot. Have you seen him, Miss Spencer?"

"I thought I heard a noise out here a few moments ago," Juliana replied, peering into the shadows.

"Faustus," Melody called again and was rewarded a second later as the sheepdog bounded out from behind one of the statues.

Dysart watched as the ladies tugged and coaxed Faustus safely into the library. When Miss Spencer disappeared from his view, he stretched, brushed futilely at the dog hairs covering his pantaloons, and then sauntered toward the other guests.

He encountered his secretary a few moments later in the small salon.

Charles took one look at him and murmured, "I was wondering where you'd got to, my lord, but I apprehend you have been visiting the kennels."

Dysart glanced down and cursed silently. Black and white hairs showed vividly against the buff color of his pantaloons. He tried brushing them off, but it was amazing the way the hair that had shed so easily from the dog clung so stubbornly to him. If Miss Spencer saw him in this condition, she was certain to realize he'd been on the terrace with that blasted sheepdog. She had too quick a mind not to make the connection.

"Shall I order the carriage brought around, sir?" Charles asked, and though he sounded sympathetic, humor lurked in his eyes.

Dysart shook his head. The notion was tempting, but he could not simply disappear without taking leave of his hostess. And he knew that if he sought out Mrs. Throckmorton, he ran the risk of meeting Miss Spencer. Much as he loathed the idea, only one solution came to mind.

Ignoring his secretary's amusement, he muttered, "We shall leave within the hour, Charles, but there is something I must do first. I shall see you later."

Dysart found a footman stationed in the hall and asked directions to the kitchen.

"To the kitchen, my lord?" the man asked, understandably astonished. "Is there something I can fetch for you?"

"Thank you, but I wish to see someone there—if you would just tell me the way, I would appreciate it," Dysart replied, pressing a coin into the man's hand.

"Very good, sir. I shall direct you myself."

It was just as well he did, Dysart thought, for the footman led them through a series of long, meandering hallways before emerging into the cavernous room that served Blandings. He left Dysart at the door.

The bustle and preparation in the kitchen came to a halt as one after another of the servants noticed the young lord standing by the door. It was the rotund chef who finally came forward. "May I be of assistance, sir?"

But Dysart had already spotted the sheepdog, hovering near one of the long tables, unashamedly begging for a leftover bone. Reluctantly, but knowing it had to be done, Dysart forced a smile to his lips and called, "Faustus, here boy."

As the dog bounded toward him, he glanced at the chef. "I could not leave without saying hello to my old friend here." As if to confirm his words, he knelt and allowed Faustus to greet him with all the fervor of his breed. His visit would not go unremarked.

Chapter 4

Charles Harrington, his solid, dependable bulk wedged into a comfortable chair on Monday morning, observed Lord Dysart for several moments without speaking. Then, his gray eyes filled with concern, hesitantly inquired, "Is there something troubling you, my lord?"

He knew it was impertinent of him to ask, and unlikely that his lordship would confide in him, but he was at a loss to know what else to do. Three times Lord Dysart had begun dictating a letter, and three times his lordship's words had tapered off into silence.

"I beg your pardon?" Dysart said, looking around absently. "Did you say something, Charles?"

"Nothing of importance, my lord."

The earl tossed his letter on the desk. "I cannot seem to concentrate on correspondence today. What say we pay a courtesy call on Mrs. Throckmorton? We should thank her for her hospitality on Friday."

"If you wish, sir," Charles replied.

"I wish . . . never mind. Have the carriage brought around. I shall be out directly."

"Very good, my lord," Charles said and discreetly withdrew.

For some moments, Dysart continued to sit at his desk, his gaze again riveted on the window, though he saw nothing of the sweeping lawns or meticulously kept gardens beyond the library. He wished he could erase the image of Miss Spencer from his mind, but he could not. The man had claimed she'd stolen some jewels. Dysart didn't believe it. Her instant denial had held the ring of truth—she'd been too indignant and too ready to face her accuser. The earl prided himself on his ability to judge people, and his instinct told him Miss Spencer was not the sort to run a rig . . . but that same instinct also warned him that she was not the innocent companion she pretended to be.

If he had any sense, he thought, he would forget the entire conversation he'd overheard and let Miss Spencer sort out her own problems. He could return to Town and amuse himself with the new actress in Drury Lane. But even as the notion occurred to him, Dysart knew he would not act on it. No lady should have to face a man like Snelling alone, and it appeared Miss Spencer had no one to turn to for help.

The thought brought a smile to his lips. The role of knight errant did not sit easily on his shoulders. He was far more accustomed to seducing ladies than protecting them. Miss Spencer needed someone like Dysart's cousin James, solid and reliable. James was a pillar of respectability and had been held up to Dysart as a pattern card for as long as he could recollect. James would know what to do. . . . Dysart tried to imagine his cousin's reaction had he been the one to overhear Miss Spencer's conversation, then shook his head.

Even if James so far forgot himself as to eavesdrop on a lady's conversation, he would undoubtedly recommend she be turned over to the authorities or left to her own devices. What was needed, Dysart thought, was a gentleman chivalrous enough to protect a lady, but not *entirely* virtuous. With dismay, he realized he was describing himself.

The notion was unsettling. He rose reluctantly and strode outside to meet his secretary. How the devil was he to help the lady if she would not confide in him? Perhaps it would be best to simply approach Snelling at the inn, pay the fellow off, and be rid of him ... only that was not likely to be the end of it. Miss Spencer would still be at the mercy of the next runner Lucian sent after her—whoever Lucian might be.

Frustrated, he climbed into the waiting carriage. He needed to know more if he was to help Miss Spencer, and yet he doubted she would trust him sufficiently to tell him the truth. Nor was it likely she would appreciate knowing he had spied on her, however innocent his motives. Sprawled in the corner of the carriage, it was several moments before he noticed Charles regarding him gravely. Dysart sat up, adjusted his cravat, and asked, "Have I suddenly grown two heads?"

"No, my lord," his secretary replied with a smile. "It is only that you seem unusually preoccupied. Is there aught I can do?"

"Thank you, but no. Well, perhaps there is. Should the opportunity arise, I would like a few words with Miss Spencer in private. If you could contrive to keep Miss Montague occupied—," he broke off his words as his secretary lifted his brows and chuckled out loud. "Pray enlighten me, Charles. What is it you find so amusing?"

"It seems only a few days ago that you warned me to forget Miss Montague, and I believe I recall your saying you intended to heed your own advice and—"

"I know precisely what I said," Dysart interrupted, "and it was excellent advice. However, I am not asking you to wed the girl but only to speak to her for a few moments. Of course, I quite understand if you feel that is beyond your capability?"

Chastened, Charles replied soberly, "No, my lord. I should be pleased to do whatever possible to assist you."

Dysart looked at him suspiciously. "If it is truly your

ambition to rise in political circles, you would do well to cultivate a less exacting memory."

"Yes, my lord," Charles said, just as though he had not had occasion in the past to forget the numerous females entertained in Dysart's home or the perfumed billets he had discreetly conveyed to his lordship from certain married ladies.

The ladies at Blandings were receiving in the blue drawing room, and it appeared to Lord Dysart that half the young gentlemen in the county had called—and more than a few of the young ladies. He paused in the doorway, surveying the assembled throng. Mrs. Throckmorton sat on the cream-colored sofa at the far end of the room, with several other matrons of similar age grouped about her. Near the windows, Miss Melody Throckmorton and her cousin, Miss Damaris Montague, occupied a loveseat, surrounded by half a dozen admiring beaus. A number of less fortunate girls were seated at intervals along the south wall, along with their attendant suitors and watchful mamas. On the opposite side of the room, Oliver Throckmorton stood by the fireplace with several of his cronies, covertly eyeing the young ladies.

When Wilfred, the butler, announced their arrival, it seemed to Dysart that every eye in the room swiveled in their direction. His hostess beamed a warm welcome, her daughter nodded shyly, and Miss Montague bestowed upon them the complacent sort of smile that said she was not at all surprised to see them. Several of the gentlemen looked less than pleased, and a few young ladies intrigued. For the beat of several seconds, all conversation ceased.

It resumed abruptly as Dysart crossed the room to pay his respects to Mrs. Throckmorton. But even as he stood chatting with the lady and her companions, Mrs. Chadleigh and the vicar's wife, Mrs. Trilby, he was aware of a keen sense of disappointment. Miss Spencer was not in the room.

"Do you not think so, my lord?" Mrs. Throckmorton said, her piercing voice breaking into his thoughts.

"Yes, indeed," he murmured, without the least notion of what he was agreeing to.

"I told you so," Mrs. Throckmorton crowed triumphantly to her friends. "Miss Spencer said the same, and she, you know, may be relied upon entirely when it comes to matters of taste."

"Breeding shows, I always say," Mrs. Chadleigh agreed. "Miss Spencer is certainly a gem. I only wonder that she has never wed."

"She has no dowry," Mrs. Throckmorton reminded her friend, lowering her voice to a loud whisper. "There are unfortunate circumstances in her past, I believe, but we do not speak of it." She raised her voice, concluding, "But surely we must be boring his lordship with such trivial conversation."

"Not at all," Dysart declaimed. "But where is Miss Spencer? I do hope her efforts in organizing the party did not exhaust her?"

"Good heavens, no," Mrs. Throckmorton said with a wry laugh. "Of course, I made most of the arrangements myself. Miss Spencer merely carried out my orders, which is not nearly so tiring as trying to think of everything that must be done. I declare if anyone is exhausted, it is I. Why, I have barely the strength to sit here, but Miss Spencer finds such idleness too tame. She is strolling in the garden with Miss Trilby."

"She is just like my daughter," the vicar's wife confided with a touch of maternal pride. "Dear Pamela can never abide to be still for long. She must always be doing something."

Having learned what he wished to know from his hostess, Dysart thanked her warmly for her kind invitation, then, under the pretext of wishing to pay his respects to the younger ladies, begged leave to be excused. He was aware that Miss Montague had been watching him for some moments, but as he approached the corner where she held court, he saw her deliberately turn and engage one of her suitors in conversation.

Amused, he ignored her and spoke to Melody. "Miss Throckmorton, may I say you look delightfully charming? One would not guess you had danced until the small hours of the morning."

"Thank you, my lord," she replied, her cheeks a rosy pink, and added naively, "You do not look like it, either."

Damaris muttered, "Oh, for heaven's sake. One does not say such a thing to a gentleman." Casting an arch glance at Dysart, she continued, "Besides, his lordship is from London. He is, no doubt, accustomed to attending balls every night of the week and staying out until dawn more nights than not."

Dysart grinned. With a hint of mischief dancing in his dark eyes, he replied, "I confess to keeping late hours, Miss Montague, but I rarely attend any balls. My evenings are usually spent, uh, . . . more intimately."

The young lady reddened but Melody gazed innocently up at him. "With a few friends, do you mean? I always think a small group more pleasant. One is so much more comfortable with just one's particular friends."

Damaris gave an abrupt laugh. "I doubt that is what his lordship meant—"

"Oh, but it is," Dysart interrupted. "Precisely so. Indeed, I was just thinking this room vastly overcrowded. Would you care to take a turn around the garden with me, Miss Throckmorton?"

"I?" Melody asked, looking both surprised and flattered. When Dysart nodded, she rose to her feet and accepted his arm, then glanced hesitantly back at her cousin. Lowering her voice, she suggested, "Perhaps we should ask Damaris to join us?"

Dysart glanced over his shoulder and nearly choked at the look of enraged fury on Miss Montague's face. She would never allow her younger cousin to provide her an escort. He smiled down at Melody and said, loud enough for Damaris to hear, "I think Miss Montague would prefer to remain inside with her coterie of admirers."

He caught his secretary's eye as they crossed to the terrace doors, and a moment later Charles joined them. The trio strolled outside, talking inconsequentially of the party.

Melody looked up at the earl and confided shyly, "Mama thought it a trifle strange that you went down to the kitchens just to see Faustus on Friday, but I thought it extremely kind. You must be very fond of dogs."

"Indeed, yes, and yours is such a likable creature. I don't believe I have ever seen another quite like him. Have you, Charles?"

"No, my lord. He is an Original, I believe."

"Thank you both. Faustus is not purebred, of course, but I do think he has a great deal of character. What kind of dog do you own, my lord?"

Dysart looked taken aback, but he recovered swiftly. "There are, uh, several in my kennels. Mostly bloodhounds."

"But surely you have a pet in the house?"

"Well, no. I—I am at Windward so seldom, I did not think it would be fair to keep a dog there."

She patted his arm consolingly. "Never mind. I shall share Faustus with you while you are here. You may come walk him whenever you please."

Charles choked on a burst of laughter, which he turned into a convincing fit of coughing. While Miss Throckmorton turned to him compassionately, Dysart made a mental note to strangle Charles at the first opportunity.

56

However, his secretary redeemed himself a few moments later when Miss Spencer approached, her arm linked with Miss Trilby's.

After greetings were exchanged, Charles, using all the persuasive skills at his command, managed to walk off with both Miss Trilby and Miss Throckmorton, leaving his employer alone with Miss Spencer.

Dysart offered the lady his arm and they strolled slowly toward the house. What did one say in such a situation? he wondered. *Afternoon, Miss Spencer. By the way, if you need assistance dealing with a blackmailer, I'm at your service.* Wishing he possessed some of his secretary's diplomacy, he managed to inquire after her health. When she returned a prosaic answer, he remarked, "Mrs. Throckmorton seems well pleased with her party, but I suspect much of the credit should go to you. Have you often arranged such affairs?"

"As the occasion requires. Mrs. Throckmorton very much enjoys having guests sit down to dinner," she replied evasively.

"And you, Miss Spencer? You seem so adept, I can only imagine you must have entertained a great deal in your own home."

She smiled wistfully. "No ... I think that after my mother died, my father lacked the heart."

"I am very sorry," Dysart murmured.

Juliana glanced up at him. The warm sympathy in his eyes melted a little of her reserve. "Thank you. 'Twas a difficult time, but not entirely unhappy. My brother and I were left on our own, but we were content to have it so."

"I think it must be rare to hear a young lady speak so well of her brother. My experience has been that most families argue incessantly."

Amused, Juliana replied, "Have you no sisters, my lord?"

"Fortunately, no. I am an only child, and therefore

made much of by my parents. No brothers or sisters to divert their attention."

"You would feel differently had you a sister. I adored my brother. Of course we argued, but . . . he was always there when I needed him, ready to fight my battles for me, bail me out of trouble, or warn off any gentleman who presumed too much."

He watched her as she spoke, admiring the way her eyes changed from cool blue to shimmering green, but this was no time for dalliance. He probed for more information, remarking casually, "Your brother sounds like a paragon. Where is he now?"

The change in her was perceptible. The long lashes swept down, hiding her expressive eyes, her back stiffened slightly, and her voice was noticeably cool as she replied, "He died two years ago. Why are you so interested in my past, my lord?"

Dysart sought to regain the ground he had lost. "One might as well ask why the stars are admired, or a particular sunrise. You are a lovely young lady, Miss Spencer. Surely other gentlemen have expressed an interest? Wished to know more about you?"

"I am a paid companion, my lord. I have no dowry, and no prospects, which puts me in a class of ladies quite beneath your notice. I suggest you practice your charm on someone more receptive. Pray excuse me."

On Wednesday morning, Lord Dysart allowed his valet to help him on with his riding coat and boots, and to make a last adjustment to his stock. Then, wishing a few minutes alone to consider the situation, he dismissed Roberts. Although the earl had dined twice at Blandings and astutely questioned both Miss Throckmorton and Miss Montague, he had learned very little more about Miss Spencer. Time was running out. Snelling had said he would return on Friday at midnight, and Dysart still had no plan. Nor was he any closer to winning Miss Spencer's confidence.

Other gentlemen might have been daunted by the lack of progress and the lady's very definite coolness, but Dysart remained determined to help—whether Miss Spencer wanted his assistance or not. Despite the manner in which she had brushed him off, he had learned two very important facts. Both her mother and her brother had recently died, and, judging by her present situation, he suspected her father was dead as well. It seemed a logical assumption that her father's estate had been entailed, and passed to some remote relative in the male line—the mysterious Lucian, perhaps? That would account for her straitened circumstances.

He wished his mother were in Town. Although French herself, she possessed an endless fascination with the lineage of every notable family in England. She could probably reel off the names of several young ladies who, due to the inheritance laws, had suddenly found themselves penniless. He should have listened more carefully to her lectures. A few years ago, when she was actively trying to coax him into matrimony, his mother had pointed out that if anything were to happen to him, a remote cousin living in America would inherit not only the title but all their lands.

Dysart had cared little. After all, he'd reasoned, if he was dead, why should he worry about the entail? Annoyed, his mother had finally given up her matchmaking efforts. Perhaps, Dysart mused, it was just as well *Maman* was abroad. Were he to suddenly start inquiring about young ladies, she would be certain to imagine a wedding in the offing.

He supposed one day in the future, he would marry and produce enough little Kinboroughs to gladden his mother's heart. But not now. He enjoyed his bachelor life too much to become legshackled, and he had sufficient time. To hear Maman talk, he was rapidly declining into old age, but he would not turn thirty until next August. Plenty of time yet. . . .

He glanced up at a discreet tap and saw his secretary peering around the bedchamber door.

"My lord, have you forgot we are riding this morning?"

"No, but thank you, Charles. I shall be down directly."

After his secretary withdrew, Dysart picked up his gloves and riding crop and stepped in front of the looking glass. He removed a tiny feather from the sleeve of his burgundy coat. Satisfied, he strode down the hall. Miss Spencer might spurn his company, but Mrs. Throckmorton was pleased to welcome him whenever he chose to call, as were her daughter and Miss Montague. The little heiress had agreed with alacrity when Dysart proposed they go riding today. He had only suggested it because he knew Miss Spencer would go along as chaperon. He supposed he should feel guilty for using Miss Montague in such a manner, but he felt certain she had agreed only to make her other suitors jealous.

His suspicions were confirmed a short while later when he cantered into the courtyard at Blandings. At least a dozen young men and women were either mounted or walking their horses as they waited for their hostess. He recognized the trio that habitually trailed after Miss Montague, two of Oliver's particular friends, and several ladies he'd met at the ball.

Dysart, his dark brows arching upward, reined in beside Miss Spencer. "I had thought this a simple afternoon ride, but it looks more like the start of a foxhunt. All we need is the master and the hounds—ah, I beg your pardon, I see the hounds *are* represented."

Juliana glanced toward the house. She could not quite suppress a smile as Faustus bounded out the door, followed only a trifle more sedately by Melody. The young

60

girl turned back to say something, and a second later her cousin emerged. It was obvious the two had been arguing, but Damaris was all smiles the instant she realized she had an audience. So like her to keep everyone waiting while she made an entrance.

With a sigh, Juliana said, "If you will excuse me, my lord, I shall try to hurry my charges." She handed the reins of the handsome roan to a waiting groom and strode toward the house.

Dysart watched the little heiress as she halted on the steps, apparently searching for someone in the courtyard—or giving those assembled the opportunity to admire her. More likely the latter, he thought cynically, but he had to admit that riding attire suited the girl. Her habit, a deep blue, brought out the color of her eyes. Decorated in the military style with a lot of heavy black braid, it had the effect of making Damaris appear extremely feminine. Or perhaps it was the tiny hat perched on her blond curls, with its absurd blue feathers, that made her look so enchantingly female.

"Beautiful, is she not?" Charles murmured.

The reverence in his secretary's voice disturbed Dysart, and he turned to quietly warn him. "Lightly over the fences, Charles!"

"I am aware Miss Montague is above my touch, my lord, but one cannot help admiring her loveliness."

Dysart grinned. "Come down off your high horse. It's you I am concerned about. Financial considerations aside, I doubt the chit worthy of you. She is indeed beautiful, but I suspect she thinks only of herself."

Charles stiffened slightly. "I believe you misjudge her, my lord. I have come to know her better these last few days. Miss Montague is headstrong, yes, and craves attention, but only because she has never experienced the natural concern and care of a close family." Before his employer could object, Charles nudged his horse and cantered toward the drive.

Bemused, Dysart stared after him. He had thought his secretary too sensible to fall for a pretty face. This was a complication he had not looked for and one he would have to do something about. He was fond of Charles, too fond to allow his secretary to be hurt by a thoughtless, shallow creature like Damaris Montague.

He watched as Miss Spencer spoke quietly to the girl, who then floated slowly down the steps and crossed the drive. Several of her suitors rushed forward to assist her to mount, but it was Charles who gave her a leg up.

"My lord?"

Dysart looked round, startled. Miss Throckmorton, lost in the shadow of her cousin's beauty, had crossed the yard without his noticing and stood waiting to speak to him. Looking down into her heart-shaped face and large, brown eyes, he thought again that she was the very girl for Charles. They were ideally suited—but neither had the sense to realize it. Smiling at her, he said, "Good afternoon, Miss Throckmorton. Are you riding today?"

She shook her head. "No, but Mr. Chadleigh is going to drive me in his curricle. We shall follow you as far as the high meadow, then turn back."

"We could stay on the road if you like," Dysart offered.

"Oh, no. Damaris loves to jump the fences up there and I would not spoil her pleasure for the world, only . . ."

"Only?" he prompted.

Melody's fair skin took on a becoming tinge of pink. "Damaris says I should not ask it of you, and I would not, but I know how fond you are of Faustus, and I truly did not think you would mind. . . ." She paused, taking a deep breath, then continued in a rush, "He does so love a good run. If it would not be a terrible imposition . . ."

"My dear Miss Throckmorton, I am yours to command. Ask away. What is it you wish me to do?"

"Thank you, my lord. You are most obliging, and it is really very little. If you would just keep an eye on Faustus? Generally he is quite good and will follow the horses, but sometimes he does chase rabbits, and I so fear he will get lost."

Dysart glanced at the shaggy sheepdog sitting patiently at her feet and hid a smile. If Faustus was in any danger, it was from being overfed. Pampered, petted, and spoiled, it was highly unlikely the dog would stray. But Dysart gallantly gave his promise and was rewarded by a blinding smile of gratitude before Miss Throckmorton joined Mr. Chadleigh in his curricle.

"Come along, Faustus," Dysart urged. Miss Spencer was organizing the riders and could do with some help.

As he approached, Miss Montague batted her long lashes and smiled coquettishly at him. "My lord, I do hope you are not too disappointed that we will not be riding alone. When some of my friends heard we were going, they simply insisted on joining us."

"Not at all, my dear," he returned, nodding at the others. "But you lead off with your friends. I wish a word with Miss Spencer."

Miffed, Damaris turned her showy chestnut stallion and trotted to the head of the drive. She handled the horse well, light hands on the reins, good seat, and back straight as a board. But there had been a look in her eyes that boded ill.

Watching her charge, Juliana shook her head at Dysart. "Must you provoke her?"

"Did I?"

"Of course. You must know she expected you to express your disappointment that you are not her only escort. Now she will ride neck or nothing just to show you

63

how little she cares. I only hope she may not take a spill and break an arm or leg."

"We should be so fortunate," he murmured.

Juliana's cool gaze met his. "Is that jealousy speaking, my lord?"

"Hardly," Dysart said with a laugh. "Miss Montague is a spoiled little girl—not at all the sort of female to attract my attention."

"Then I wonder that you asked her to go riding."

"It was the only way I could think of to have a word alone with you."

Her turquoise eyes flashed fire. Charles might think Miss Montague a beauty, but in Dysart's opinion she could not hold a candle to Juliana Spencer. Her high cheekbones were tinged with just a blush of pink, and the small, upturned nose lifted a fraction as she stared at him. Her auburn hair was drawn up beneath her riding hat, but coppery tendrils caressed her neck and caught the glint of the sun. He would like to see it tumbled about her shoulders. . . .

"I have told you, Lord Dysart, that—"

"As a paid companion you are beneath my notice," he interrupted, finishing the sentence for her. "But I do notice you, and I should like to be friends."

One could not doubt the sincerity in his voice. Surprised, she turned her gaze away. "I . . . I do not know what to say."

"Then try, 'Thank you, my lord. I should like very much to be friends with you.' Because, my dear Miss Spencer, I think you could use a friend."

Flustered, she kept her eyes fixed on the others. The riders ahead of them had turned off the road and were heading across the high meadow, Damaris leading the way, Oliver and Charles just behind her.

"What do you say, Miss Spencer? Shall we cry friends?"

"Oh, bloody hell," she muttered, and kneed her horse, sending her galloping across the field.

For a second, Dysart thought he had been spurned. Then he heard Oliver's shout and looked across the field. Damaris was rushing the jump—a four-foot-high stone wall. She could not possibly get her horse up in time.

Chapter 5

Juliana raced across the field. Her own horse, a well-mannered gray mare, was a suitable mount for a lady but no match for the high-strung chestnut stallion Damaris rode. Oliver had warned his cousin that the horse was too much for her to handle, and, of course, Damaris had immediately insisted on purchasing the animal. She took a great deal of pride in her riding ability and would never own that any horse was beyond her capability.

Now the stallion had bolted or else she'd deliberately given him his head in an effort to show off her superb horsemanship—only this time the effect might misfire. If she didn't get her horse up in time . . . Juliana, her heart in her throat, breathed a silent prayer. Then she heard the pounding of hooves and glanced behind her. Lord Dysart's champion black closed the distance between them rapidly. She had a glimpse of the horse's long legs and flashing stride as he swept past. But even Conqueror could not reach Damaris in time.

The tableau before Juliana would remain forever fixed in her mind, so much was it at odds with the danger before them. The riders were spread out, their coats vivid splashes of color across the lush greenness of the meadow. Here and there, patches of bright yellow buttercups dotted the field, and beneath the trees she could see the bluish purple of periwinkles. The sun shimmered against the sheen of a horse's coat and cast long shadows beneath the scattered trees. Ahead stood the old stone wall, built by the Romans, now gray and weather-beaten, but still solid.

The impressions were fleeting. Juliana trained her gaze on Damaris and the chestnut. The horse rose majestically from the ground, arcing upward, and for one magnificent second was highlighted against the blue of the sky. Then he vaulted over the wall and disappeared from her sight. She heard cries of relief from those nearer and saw Dysart's stallion sail over the wall in Damaris's wake.

Charles and Oliver drew rein and dismounted. As Juliana approached, they made for the rusted iron gate and strode through, leading their horses. She could see Damaris now, still mounted, laughing at everyone's concern. Her own hands shaking, Juliana breathed deeply, then guided Ladyslipper through the open gate.

"Of all the idiotic stunts," Oliver was shouting at his cousin. "I know you've more hair than wit, but even you should have better sense than to rush a fence like that."

"I jumped it cleanly, did I not?" Damaris retorted. "Good heavens, I do not see what all the fuss is about. I know what I'm doing."

"You might have broken the horse's leg—did you think of that?"

"But the point is I did not. Really, Oliver, you have seen me ride often enough to know I could take a jump like this in my sleep." She turned and appealed to Dysart. "You were just behind me, my lord. Tell him I judged the wall perfectly."

"You rushed it," Dysart replied uncompromisingly. "And if you are asking my opinion, Miss Montague, I think only a fool or a novice would risk a horse in so rash a manner."

"I noticed that you did not hesitate at the wall, my lord," she replied, nettled by his attitude.

"I wanted to be here to pick up the pieces—or to put the horse down, if necessary. Since neither is required, pray excuse me."

Pamela Trilby came through the gate on foot, leading her horse. "Oh, Damaris, thank the good Lord you are unharmed. You frightened me half to death. I quite thought you had misjudged the . . ." Her words trailed off as she realized her friend, whom she adored, was glaring and not at all appreciative of her concern.

Damaris forced a small laugh and tossed her head. "Well, I had not realized this was such a fainthearted group! Perhaps I should return home and leave all of you to trot tamely around the meadow?" Anger heightened the color of her cheeks and her gaze swept scathingly across the riders.

"That would suit me just fine," Oliver snapped.

Juliana nudged her horse to draw even with her charge and said with quiet neutrality, "If you wish to return home, Damaris, I shall accompany you. Indeed, I think that might be best."

"Oh, please do not," Pamela cried, her protest echoed by several of the others. "Why, we have not been out above an hour."

Damaris glanced at the circle surrounding her. She had expected her cousin to be annoyed—Oliver hated it that she could ride better than he—and, of course, Miss Spencer never approved of anything she did. But she was surprised that Lord Dysart, whom she thought would be a neck-or-nothing rider, had spoken so rudely. Worse, Patrick Fitzhugh studiously avoided her eyes, and Charlotte Chadleigh seemed inordinately interested in soothing her horse.

68

Damaris shifted her gaze to Charles Harrington. Stuffy, dependable Charles. She had thought he liked her. His eyes followed her wherever she went . . . but now he was staring at her with marked disapproval—or disappointment. Well, she didn't care what he thought of her, what any of them thought. Her chin lifted and her eyes glittered. Dangerously close to tears, she bit her lip. Who were these people, these provincials, to judge her? She didn't need them. She'd promised to meet Cressy Milhouse a little further on, and Cressy would not condemn her for intrepidly taking a jump the others were too cowardly to try. Nor would Andrew Marling. *He* was game for anything and had promised to try to come with Cressy. They were to "accidentally" meet near the church ruins. She would not ride tamely home now.

Assuming a chastened air she was far from feeling, Damaris turned to her companion. "Miss Spencer, I am most sorry that everyone was alarmed, and I should truly hate to spoil the others' pleasure. May we please continue? I promise to hold Midnight to a canter and to follow my cousin's lead over the jumps."

Juliana nodded reluctantly. Although every sense told her Damaris was planning some devilment, there was little she could say amid the chorus of approval without embarrassing the girl further.

"An excellent compromise," Charles Harrington declared and moved alongside Damaris. "You do realize, Miss Montague, that we are only concerned for your well-being? I will say that, although you should not have attempted it, 'twas nevertheless a splendid jump."

"How kind of you," Damaris murmured. And though Mr. Harrington was not the sort of gentleman she admired, she could not help feeling just a little bit pleased by his praise.

Juliana, dropping back to ride alongside Dysart, heard the exchange and wondered at the gullibility of certain men. Let a pretty girl bat her lashes and they seemed to lose all their usual good sense—even someone she knew to be usually levelheaded and intelligent like Mr. Harrington. She glanced at Lord Dysart beside her. He at least did not seem smitten, but she thought she would almost prefer that to the cynicism that twisted his mouth into a wry grin.

"Someone needs to take a birch rod to Miss Montague and paddle some sense into her head."

Juliana frequently felt the same. However, she understood why Damaris always felt it necessary to be the center of attention, and although she deplored the girl's behavior, she still hated to hear someone else criticize her. She smiled ruefully, "Were you beaten often as a child, my lord?"

He looked startled. "No, of course not. If anything, I suppose my parents rather spoiled me."

She was not surprised. He had that air of self-confidence that comes only when a person knows they are truly valued. Oliver possessed it, too. Melody was not as self-assured, but she had been very young when her father died. It did make a difference, Juliana thought. . . .

"Come back, Miss Spencer," Dysart said. When she glanced at him, he grinned. "Being the only child of devoted parents, I am accustomed to having one's full attention. You looked a hundred miles away. What were you thinking about?"

"Of Damaris, I suppose, and childhoods. She was orphaned at an early age and passed from relative to relative, most of whom only wanted her because of the fortune she inherited."

"A pity, but I hardly think it an excuse for a lack of common sense. I gather from what little you have said about your past, that you, too, were orphaned. Yet, I would wager you'd never be tempted to rush a fence so recklessly."

70

She laughed. "No, my lord, but that may be due more to cowardice than good sense."

His brows lifted. "I doubt you ever behave in a cowardly fashion, Miss Spencer."

"Thank you," she replied, wondering at the odd note in his voice. "But I fear you do not know me well enough to judge."

"We could remedy that."

Lord, he had a smile that would charm any female from six to sixty. Avoiding his eyes, she leaned forward to pet Ladyslipper's neck. "My lord, I—"

"I am only suggesting we become better acquainted, Miss Spencer. I know so little about you."

"There is very little to know. I am a paid companion and, at the moment, guilty of neglecting my duties. I should be riding with Damaris."

"Leave her to Charles," he advised. "I suspect that at the moment she would much prefer his company, and she is perfectly safe with him."

"I did not mean to imply otherwise, my lord, but Damaris is my responsibility."

"And you never neglect your duties?" he asked, a teasing note in his voice. "What an extraordinary upbringing you must have had. One that imbued you with all the most respectable virtues. Did your parents beat you?"

She couldn't help laughing. "No, my lord, but perhaps they should have. I assure you, I am not nearly so virtuous as you seem to think."

"Now that is promising," he said with a mock leer. "What virtues are you lacking?"

"Many, I promise you," she replied and nudged her horse to quicken the pace. They were drifting farther and farther behind the others. Lord Dysart did not seem to notice, but she knew her behavior was hardly suitable for a chaperon. She could imagine what the gossips would say: My dear, did you hear the latest? Miss Spencer is setting her cap for the earl. When they were riding the other day, she spent all of her time with his lordship. . . .

"May I ask you one question, Miss Spencer?"

"You have already asked a great many, my lord. I suggest we join the others."

"One of my worst faults is an insatiable curiosity—"

"I am surprised you own to any faults."

He grinned, unabashed. "My mother would provide you with a list a yard long. She never fails to bring up all my shortcomings when I visit."

"I think I would like your mother."

"She would certainly like you. I believe she would approve of anyone who agrees with her that I am less than perfection. I'm afraid I am in her black book just at present."

She glanced at him. The words were light, teasing, and she could not discern if there was any truth in them. But there had been something in his voice . . . she couldn't help wondering if Dysart's mother was annoyed because of the rumors about him. Even living retired as she did, Juliana had heard tales of his scandalous reputation.

"Egad, I would love to know what's running through that pretty head of yours! Did anyone ever tell you that you have the most expressive eyes? The look on your face—but you may relax, Miss Spencer. I haven't seduced the vicar's daughter or trifled with one of the housemaids, if that is what you are thinking. Maman is upset with me only because I have yet to set up housekeeping. She merely has a strong yearning to dangle a grandchild on her knee."

"Your mother sounds delightful and I should like to hear more of her, but the others—" She gestured with her riding crop. Some twenty yards ahead, the rest of the party were approaching the first of several fences.

"We can easily catch them," Dysart said. "I shall even race you to the fence if you will answer one question for me."

"Does your mother include stubbornness among your faults, my lord?" she asked, exasperated. When he continued only to grin, she said, "Very well. One question only, sir. What is it you wish to know?"

"Where are you from? I have been racking my brains to think why your voice sounds familiar. I suspect a northern influence. Am I right?"

"Cumberland," she conceded, then kneed Ladyslipper, gaining a length on Dysart before he realized the race was on. As she rode, she watched Damaris, riding between Charles and Oliver, take the first fence easily. Unfortunately, her own gentle mare proved no match for Conqueror's long legs. He swept past her and was over the fence while she was still two lengths back.

Dysart reined in, turned, and waited while Juliana brought her mount easily over the low fence. He called Faustus to heel beside him, then said, "Well done, Miss Spencer. Who taught you to ride—your brother?"

More questions, Juliana thought warily. Was it mere curiosity on Dysart's part or something more? She forced a smile and replied lightly, "I agreed to one question, my lord, which I answered. Now, I must see to Damaris."

"She can come to no harm among her friends," Dysart argued persuasively. "Did you not see how sweetly she took the fence?"

"I am more worried about her choice of companions," Juliana answered and nodded toward the group of young people. They'd reined in and were waiting beneath the trees for two other riders now cutting across the field from the east. Even from this distance, she recognized the pair. "I should have suspected Damaris was up to mischief. The young lady is Miss Milhouse and her escort is Andrew Marling, a gentleman whose attentions my employer very much wishes to discourage. Hurry, my lord."

Racing across the field, Dysart and Juliana joined the others a few moments later. As she drew her mare to a halt, Damaris greeted her with a sweetly innocent smile.

"Miss Spencer, is it not wonderful? We chanced upon Cressy and Mr. Marling. I knew you would not object if they joined us."

From behind her, Juliana heard Dysart's low voice murmur, "I still think a birch rod would be advisable."

"How utterly charming you look, Miss Spencer," Andrew Marling drawled as he stepped forward. His hazel eyes gleamed defiantly. He knew quite well he was not welcome, but his triumphant smile and swaggering stance dared Juliana to do anything about it.

Faustus, his short back legs braced, took exception to Mr. Marling's tone and barked at the interloper until Dysart called the sheepdog to his side.

"Why do you dislike the gentleman so much?" Lord Dysart asked late that afternoon as they cantered down the lane leading to Blandings.

"Mrs. Throckmorton does not wish to offer him any encouragement," Juliana replied tactfully. It had taken all of her skills, and most of her attention, to keep Damaris and Andrew Marling separated. She was tired and annoyed with her charge for once again spoiling what might have been a pleasant afternoon.

"Naturally. 'Tis well known he's hanging out for an heiress, but your dislike seems to go beyond the natural concern of a chaperon, even so dutiful a one as yourself. Has he said or done something to offend you?"

"Besides his mere existence?"

74

Dysart chuckled. "I will grant that any person of discriminating taste would find him offensive, but beyond that?"

"Not really . . . but I do find him distasteful. Was it so obvious?" she asked.

"Perhaps not to everyone, but I should hate to have you look at me with such icy disdain. Now tell me, what has he done to incur your wrath?"

She knew by now that Lord Dysart would not be satisfied until he received an answer. Her patience with his "insatiable curiosity" growing thin, she retorted, "Andrew Marling is the sort of gentleman who makes chaperons necessary. His manner is patently false and one cannot believe a word he says. Nor is he above seducing a young girl if he thinks it would be to his advantage—or just for his amusement."

"Is that all?"

"All?" She turned to stare at him incredulously. "I should think that would be more than sufficient."

"Marling is an annoyance, but he can be handled—as you so adroitly demonstrated this afternoon. However, I do not believe he is the reason for those dark shadows beneath your eyes. Will you not confide in me, Miss Spencer? 'Tis possible I might be able to help."

Hearing the kindness and concern in his voice, Juliana sighed. She wished she could take advantage of his offer. Certainly, she had sufficient to worry her besides Marling's flirtation with Damaris. All week she had fretted over her meeting with the runner. Mr. Snelling would return Friday night, and she still had not come up with any plan to forestall him. If he exposed her, it would undoubtedly mean the end of her position. She would be turned away without references, without funds. . . .

She loathed the idea of selling the few pieces of jewelry her mother had left her, but she realized she had no other choice. Unfortunately, she did not have the least idea of how one went about pawning one's jewels or even selling them outright.

Eyeing Dysart speculatively, she wondered if he would know. She recalled her brother telling her how his friend Val had wagered some exceedingly large sums on Conqueror. He had won, but certainly that indicated a tendency to game heavily. At some time he must have lost. Had he ever been so hard-pressed he pawned his signet ring or the handsome gold stickpin he habitually wore? Or did he resort to a moneylender?

"Satisfied, Miss Spencer?" Dysart asked.

"I—I beg your pardon," she stammered.

"No need. Do I measure up? You were staring at me so intently, I felt you were measuring me—for a suit of armor, perhaps? I can only hope you were envisioning me as your knight errant to the rescue. I confess rescuing pretty damsels has not been much in my line, but I am willing to give it a try." He swept her a half bow from astride his horse and declared, "I am entirely at your command, fair lady."

If only it were so easy, she thought, half smiling at his nonsense. If only he could sweep her into his arms and ride off with her into the sunset. A tiny part of her reveled in the idea. Dysart had such strong arms, it would feel wonderful to . . . Abruptly, she reined in her thoughts. She had no business thinking of his lordship in such a manner. Aloud, she said, "Thank you, Lord Dysart. I apologize for my rudeness. I fear my wits were wandering. . . . 'Tis difficult to know what to do."

"My mother always says trouble shared is trouble halved."

Juliana calculated swiftly, figuring how much she could safely divulge. After a moment, she hesitantly explained, "I find myself in a somewhat embarrassing situation, my lord, in that I need fifty pounds immediately. I was wondering if you—"

"Say no more, Miss Spencer. I should be glad to give you what you need. I haven't that much on me at the moment, but in the morning—"

"Oh, no, I did not mean for *you* to give me the money, my lord," she interrupted in an agony of embarrassment, her eyes downcast. "I could not possibly accept such a gift—"

"A loan then," he proposed. "You may repay me a little each quarter day so that it will not tax your resources."

Color flooded into her face. Mortified that he would think she'd been wheedling him just to induce such an offer, she vehemently shook her head. "Thank you, Lord Dysart. 'Tis most generous of you to offer, but I cannot . . . You must see that it would be most improper of me to . . . Oh, dear, I am making a dreadful muddle of this." She took a deep breath and tried again. "I had hoped, sir, that you might tell me how one went about pawning something. I have a few pieces of jewelry left to me by my mother. If I could pawn them, or if that is not possible, sell them . . ."

"Nothing could be simpler," he assured her. "If you are certain that is what you wish, there is a goldsmith in Chichester with whom I have done some business. I am certain he would oblige me by holding your jewelry for an extended time. If you like, I could manage the business for you."

Unable to meet his gaze, she nodded.

"Consider it done, then. I shall come in for a moment and pay my respects to Mrs. Throckmorton. While we are talking, you fetch your jewels and slip them to me before I leave. I'll take care of the matter for you tomorrow, and when I come to dinner, you shall have your fifty pounds."

"Thank you," she murmured, trying to summon a smile. She should feel pleased that one of her problems had been so easily solved. Instead she felt utterly wretched.

Safely inside her bedchamber, Juliana quickly changed her riding habit for a plain muslin day dress. She did not even glance in the looking glass as she passed it, for it scarcely mattered what she looked like. She would see Lord Dysart again, of course, but after her brazen behavior today, he must think her contemptible. Certainly he would not care or even notice what she wore. Which was just as well, she resolutely told herself. There could be nothing between them beyond mere friendship, and she had probably destroyed any chance of that. Why, in heaven's name, had she asked his help?

Just because he had been kind and somehow sensed that she was troubled was no excuse. To have blurted out her immediate need for money, and in such a manner that he'd felt obliged to offer . . . the recollection of that moment filled her with shame.

She twisted off the small ruby ring that she had worn since she was fifteen. "I am sorry, Mama," she whispered as she placed it in the center of a linen handkerchief. The ruby and pearl brooch followed. Her mother had worn it every day until her death. She'd said Papa had given it to her when Philip was born. Juliana did not know if it had any monetary value, but to her it was priceless. She rubbed the silver filigree setting, slightly tarnished now.

Blinking back tears, Juliana crossed to the wardrobe and removed the tiny rosewood box. From it she withdrew the pearl ear clips Papa had given her, and added them to her other jewelry. Her fingers caressed the last of her pieces, a single strand of pearls. She hesitated, wondering if she did not have sufficient without the necklace. Then, fearful that Lord Dysart might be inclined to make up the difference if she were short, she reluctantly added the pearls to the small pile on the handkerchief. Before she could change her mind, she twisted the linen into a knot and slipped it into her pocket.

Belowstairs, she found Lord Dysart in the blue drawing room, making laborious conversation with Mrs. Throckmorton. Juliana smiled a little as she noticed Faustus sitting beside his lordship's chair, his shaggy head resting on Lord Dysart's knee.

"Oh, there you are, my dear," Mrs. Throckmorton said. "I was just trying to persuade his lordship to remain for dinner, but he fears he is abusing our hospitality. Pray tell him the notion is nonsensical. We are quite honored to have him, are we not?"

"Indeed yes," Juliana said, but she avoided looking directly at Dysart as he rose to his feet. "However, I suspect he has had sufficient of our company for one day—particularly that of Faustus. Has Melody thanked you for watching him today?"

"Several times," Dysart replied with a grin. "And I would be delighted to stay were it not for the duties I am neglecting at Windward." He turned back to Mrs. Throckmorton and extended his hand. "I really must take my leave, but if your kindness permits, might I join you tomorrow instead?"

"We would be pleased to have you, my lord. You may always be assured of finding a welcome at Blandings, and if I do say so myself, my chef sets an exceptional table."

"He does indeed—but duty calls. Until tomorrow, then." He bowed gallantly over her hand, then turned. "Miss Spencer, would you walk out with me? I fear

Faustus has developed a strong attachment for my boots and may try to follow me home."

"Certainly, my lord," she replied, her hand shaking as it closed around the knotted handkerchief in her pocket.

Chapter 6

After dinner Thursday evening, Caroline Throckmorton led the way into the blue drawing room. She settled in one of the wing chairs near the open windows, hoping to catch a cooling breeze. The sultry evening, and the large dinner she'd consumed, combined to make her feel unpleasantly lethargic. She really should not have had the cherries compote or the marzipan, she thought, remembering that Margie had had to let out the seams in her green silk gown last week, and had tactfully suggested a corset. A corset! As though she were fat instead of just the tiniest bit plump. Annoyed, Mrs. Throckmorton plied her fan vigorously and turned her attention to her niece.

Disgraceful, the way the girl had flirted with Lord Dysart during dinner. Fortunately, his lordship had chosen to be amused rather than disgusted by her brazen conduct, but something had to be done. Had Mrs. Trilby or Mrs. Fitzhugh been present, they would not have hesitated to condemn Damaris as being fast. And who would be blamed? Not the various relatives who'd had the raising of her, that was certain.

Amazing that one who looked so entirely angelic could be so full of sheer devilment, Mrs. Throckmorton thought as she motioned to her niece. "My dear, I wish a word with you. Come sit beside me."

Wary, Damaris took the chair next to her aunt. She

demurely folded her hands in her lap, sat with her back rigidly straight, and smiled sweetly. "Lord Dysart said dinner was delightful, Aunt Caroline."

"Did he, indeed? No doubt he was being kind, but even if he was amused by your conduct, I am not. You must cease flirting with every gentleman you meet, Damaris. 'Tis not at all becoming. Miss Spencer, pray tell her I speak the truth."

Juliana sighed. Damaris had that mulish look about her, her chin stubbornly set, her eyes defiant. In that mood, she was highly unlikely to listen to anything anyone had to say. It would have been better to speak to her later, in private, about behavior that more strongly resembled that of a courtesan than a properly reared young lady. But Mrs. Throckmorton was waiting.

Trying the effect of a smile and soft words, Juliana said, "Your aunt is thinking only of you, Damaris. She does not wish you to be spoken of unkindly, as you undoubtedly would be had anyone heard some of the comments you made to Lord Dysart this evening."

The girl's lower lip came out in a sulky pout. "I thought my conversation quite unexceptional."

Melody, sitting beside Miss Spencer, giggled. "Oh, Damaris, what a taradiddle. How can you say so after telling Lord Dysart that you would adore to see his rooms in Town? I could scarcely believe my ears, and Mr. Harrington nearly choked on his soup."

"Well, I *would* like to see his rooms. I have never seen a gentleman's apartment and—"

"If you think that passes for unexceptional conversation," Mrs. Throckmorton interrupted, "then you are much mistaken."

"Dysart did not mind. He thought—"

" 'Dysart'?" her aunt broke in furiously. "Lord Dysart is considerably older than you, miss, and a member of the peerage. I will thank you to speak of him in a more respectful manner."

Damaris shrugged. "Very well, but I do not understand why you should object if he does not."

"Apparently there are any number of things you fail to understand, not the least of which is conduct suitable to a young lady. Perhaps it would be better if you were excluded from dinners and other outings until you learn a measure of deportment."

"Lock me in my room, then," Damaris retorted. "I don't care."

"Damaris!" Juliana scolded. "Apologize to your aunt at once and let us hear no more of this nonsense. I know perfectly well that you are only trying to shock us all, but you go beyond the line."

Damaris tossed her head so her long mane of blond hair rippled across her shoulders. She did not look at all repentant as she murmured dutifully, "I am sorry, Aunt Caroline, for teasing you. I know I should not, but everyone seemed so dreadfully serious at dinner, I could not resist. Lord Dysart knows I was only jesting."

Mrs. Throckmorton opened her mouth to reply, but the gentlemen chose that moment to step into the room. She said no more as Lord Dysart approached, but the look she bent on her niece promised that this was not the end of their conversation.

Oliver needed only a glance at his cousin's face to realize she had been scolded for her outrageous behavior at dinner. She deserved it, but now he felt almost sorry for her and engaged her in conversation. Charles Harrington joined them, and the talk turned to horses. He could not have chosen a better topic. Damaris forgot her pose as a sophisticated young lady and talked enthusiastically about the stable she would one day have.

Juliana, her chair drawn a little to the side, paid scant attention. She'd had no opportunity to speak to Dysart alone. He had smiled at her encouragingly when he first arrived, which she took to mean that he had successfully pawned her jewels. But every time she sought a word in private with him, Damaris, Melody, or Oliver had claimed his attention. Even Faustus wanted a word from his lordship. The sheepdog sat at his heels, patiently waiting while Dysart spoke to Mrs. Throckmorton. Faustus was rewarded a moment later when his lordship obligingly scratched him behind one silky ear before making his way to Juliana's side.

"I believe this fellow would appreciate a turn about the garden," Dysart said to her. "Would you care to accompany us?"

Too relieved to think of anything clever to say, Juliana nodded. She feared the others would also join them, but just as Damaris glanced in their direction, Mr. Harrington diverted her with a question. Aware that she was truly in disgrace with her aunt, Damaris remained seated next to Melody and politely continued her conversation. And Oliver, who was beginning to idolize Dysart and would have liked very much to accompany him, was too well-bred to put himself forward. So it was that a moment later Juliana and his lordship strolled through the tall windows, her hand resting lightly on his arm, quite alone except for Faustus padding happily alongside them.

The garden was bathed in the golden light that falls between sunset and dusk, and the flowers perfumed the light breeze. Juliana never noticed. For all her eagerness to speak to his lordship in private, she suddenly found herself tongue-tied and witless. She could not just forthrightly ask him if he had pawned her jewels. Somehow it sounded so . . . so dreadfully vulgar.

Lord Dysart glanced down at her and smiled. "I am sorry, my dear, to have kept you waiting. Have you been worrying? You need not—I have excellent news for you."

She blushed, deeply embarrassed to have to discuss such tawdry business. Avoiding his gaze, she murmured, "Thank you, my lord, but I have not been so much worrying as thinking that it was most presumptuous of me to have asked your assistance."

"How odd. I have the distinct impression that it was I who offered to help you, and you who very reluctantly agreed."

"You are very kind, my lord."

"My friends call me Val," he suggested gently.

I know, she nearly answered, thinking of Philip, who had spoken so often and so warmly of Dysart. She looked up into his dark eyes and thought how easy it would be to let her guard down, to forget her present position and accept the friendship his lordship offered. For the space of a heartbeat, she longed fervently for the days when her most pressing concern was which gown to wear—those precious days when she would have been free to accept the friendship of a gentleman like Dysart. Once, she could have ridden out with him, or waltzed with him, without a thought to what others might think.

Reluctantly Juliana lowered her gaze. Those days were gone forever, and it behooved her now to remember that she was only a paid companion. Lord Dysart might disregard her position, but she could not afford to. Aloud she replied, "Thank you, my lord, but you must know it would be exceedingly inappropriate for me to address you so informally."

"I have never regarded the rules society forces on us as binding, Miss Spencer, and my friendships are not based on rank or wealth. However, as it obviously makes you uncomfortable, I will not press the issue. 'Tis only that 'my lord' makes me think of stodgy old men with large bellies who habitually suffer from gout. Do you think you might manage to just call me Dysart?"

She shook her head but couldn't help laughing. "I dare

not. After dinner, Mrs. Throckmorton roundly scolded Damaris for doing just that. You, sir, as a member of the peerage, are to be addressed with respect."

"I concede the battle, Miss Spencer," he said as they stopped near the tall hedges where Faustus was busily sniffing the ground. He withdrew a small pouch from his pocket. "I expect I had best give you this now before the others decide to join us. The jeweler said your pieces were of excellent quality, and if you should ever desire to sell them outright, he would be glad to give you a fair price, particularly for the pearls."

She slipped the small bag into her pocket without glancing at the contents.

"You are a trusting soul, my dear," Dysart said as he watched her. "Do you not wish to count your money?"

"And insult you after you have been so kind?"

"Well, do so, then, when you are alone. There are seventy-five pounds in there, my dear, along with your string of pearls. The ring and the brooch were more than sufficient."

She felt deeply grateful. After resigning herself to losing the few things of her mother's she treasured most, to have the pearls back again was a gift beyond price. When she could speak past the sudden lump in her throat, she said quietly, "I do not know how to thank you, my lord."

"As you have already done so several times in the last few moments, do not trouble yourself. But you might bear one thing in mind, Miss Spencer." He waited until she looked inquiringly up at him, then lightly brushed her cheek with the tip of his finger. "Whatever difficulty you are facing, you are not alone. I promise I shall be close by if you need me."

Friday dawned gray and rainy, effectively keeping the ladies inside, callers away, and spirits dampened. Damaris, denied permission to visit her friend Cressy

Milhouse, sulked and argued incessantly with anyone unwise enough to engage her in conversation. Shortly after noon, Mrs. Throckmorton complained of feeling out of sorts and took to her bed.

Juliana, listening to the bickering between the three younger members of the household at dinner that evening, wished that she might do the same. Eventually, however, the hands on the longcase clock in the hall inched toward nine, and, after telling Oliver for the second time that he was getting too old to tease his sister, Juliana tactfully suggested that they would all benefit from a good night's rest.

She had thought the solitude of her room would be a welcome respite, but the quiet, broken only by the sound of steadily falling rain, seemed to increase her restlessness. Her wayward thoughts wandering, she remembered Dysart's parting words and tried again to puzzle out what he had meant by them. *He would be close by if she needed him. . . .*

It sounded almost as if he knew about Snelling, which was, of course, impossible. But Dysart had sounded so concerned, so worried about her. She took momentary comfort in that, then scolded herself for being foolish. His lordship's manner was part of his natural charm, charm that had earned him a near-legendary reputation as a rake. One could not place any credence on his words. He habitually charmed every female he met, no matter the age or disposition. Melody, Mrs. Throckmorton, even Damaris, when she was not annoyed with him, found Lord Dysart irresistible. Juliana told herself his words meant nothing and that comforting a lady in distress came as naturally to him as breathing. But she could not entirely erase the image of Dysart's dark eyes shimmering with kindness as he'd offered his help.

She tried to put him from her mind, but at half past eleven she was still sitting in her chair, idly watching the wax slowly melting as the single taper she'd lit burned low. A dreadful waste, she thought, but did not extinguish the candle. She had tried to pass the hours until midnight doing mending, but after pricking her finger twice, she'd laid aside her needlework. The book she'd picked up instead, one of Hannah Moore's improving works, now lay atop her sewing. Her mind refused to concentrate on the printed words, and her thoughts strayed, first to Dysart, then to Snelling. A glance at the clock on the mantel showed it still lacked twenty minutes to the hour.

She dreaded the midnight meeting, but she was impatient to have it done with. She would pay the runner his fifty pounds, send him on his way, and pray that would be the end of the matter.

Until Lucian sent someone else.

The unwanted thought intruded, destroying what little composure she had. Refusing to think further of her despicable cousin, Juliana rose and picked up the small pouch she'd set aside for Snelling. Fifty pounds ... dearly paid for with her mother's ring and brooch. She lit another candle to carry with her, then quietly eased open the door of her bedchamber.

The long hall looked unaccountably different draped in darkness. One could easily imagine ogres hiding in the shadows. ... She flinched as a branch knocked against the casement window at the end of the hall. Telling herself not to be foolish, Juliana lifted the candle higher and crept toward the stairs.

Blandings was an old house and, like most old houses, settled for the night with a variety of unaccountable noises—but Juliana had never noticed how dreadfully the steps creaked. Each protesting groan sounded alarmingly loud to her ears. She expected Oliver or Mrs. Throckmorton to appear at any moment, demanding to know what she was about. But no one came, and her nerves steadied a little as she stepped off the last stair and turned toward the rear of the house.

Her candle flickered in the drafty hallway so that the shadows seemed to move. Why had she ever agreed to meet Snelling at midnight? She should have told him she would see him at noon in the garden, Juliana thought, as she neared the library. It had been very different coming down here last week when the house was full of guests and brightly lit.

Her heart skittered suddenly as she thought she heard a footstep ahead of her. Someone had moved, she was certain of it. She peered into the long shadows cast by the sofas and tables scattered along the hall. So many places someone could hide . . . but that was absurd. True, she had left the library windows unlatched for Snelling, but they were frequently left open at night. This was not London, where one had to worry about burglars. . . .

As she tried to convince herself it was only her imagination, Juliana tiptoed to the library door. "Mr. Snelling?" she called in a loud whisper. No one answered and although she could not see beyond a few feet, the room seemed empty. She cherished a hope that the rain had discouraged Snelling and he would not come after all . . . but she knew it still lacked a few moments till midnight. She waited a moment, then carefully set her taper down on an inlaid table. After quietly closing the door to the hall, she lit a candelabrum.

In the sudden flare of light, she saw the body.

Mr. Snelling lay sprawled on the floor just in front of the tall windows leading to the terrace. A small statue carved of black basalt normally stood on the pedestal by the window. Now it rested near Snelling's head, on top of his battered old hat. The polished stone of the statue glistened ominously in the candlelight.

Smothering an involuntary gasp, Juliana backed against the door. Her heart racing erratically, the candelabrum shaking in her hand, she gazed in horrible fascination at the inert body. "Mr. Snelling," she called again, her voice a plea that he answer or at least move.

When he remained deadly still, she crept to within a foot of the body and peered nervously down at him. It looked as though someone had surprised Snelling and bashed him over the head with the statue, perhaps thinking him an intruder. But if that was so, why had no one sounded the alarm? Juliana looked uneasily around, stifling the impulse to scream for help.

A succession of muddled thoughts flashed through her mind. How could she possibly explain her presence in the library? And if she admitted her reason for meeting the runner, would it not be natural for others to assume that she was the one who had hit him over the head?

Juliana jumped as she heard a noise on the terrace. One of the tall windows was slightly ajar—no doubt left that way when Snelling had entered. *Or left open by whoever had bashed him.* Even now someone else could be lurking outside.

Wishing that she had never made the assignation, wishing she was back in the safety of her quiet bedchamber, Juliana inched stealthily toward the terrace. She nearly dropped the candles and bolted when she heard the noise again, only she was too frightened. Agonizing seconds later, she breathed a sigh of relief as she realized the odd scraping sound was merely the wind blowing the branch of a potted shrub against the house.

Her heart slowed its frantic beat and she glanced down again at Snelling. He wore the same greatcoat he'd worn the week before, though it was now sodden with rain. He had fallen on his chest, one arm twisted beneath him, the other flung out as though to break his fall. She reluctantly set the candelabrum down and knelt beside the runner. Biting her lip, she forced herself to pick up his lifeless hand and search for a pulse.

Her mother had suffered a long, debilitating illness, and Juliana remembered the anxious nights spent by her bedside. More than once she had thought her mother had slipped away, so still, so deep was her sleep. Dr. Ingram had shown Juliana how to search for the tiny throb of life that pulsed in one's wrist.

She pulled back Snelling's worn glove and placed her fingers over the large vein. His skin was still warm to the touch, but there was no life-giving beat beneath her hand. Snelling would not trouble her again, but she took no pleasure in the knowledge. She would much rather give him all her mother's jewels than see him like this.

Juliana hesitated, uncertain what would be best to do. She quelled a strong impulse to return to her room, pack a valise, and flee into the night. The notion was tempting, for she had the seventy-five pounds Lord Dysart had given her. But she also knew that if she left in such a manner, everyone would be convinced that she was somehow responsible for Snelling's death. And he had been a runner. Bow Street would search relentlessly for whoever had murdered him.

Murdered. Just thinking the word sent a chill down her spine.

She considered rousing Oliver . . . but as she pictured the commotion *that* would ensure—the frightened maids, Mrs. Throckmorton's alarm, and the hundreds of questions she herself would undoubtedly be asked—Juliana decided that it would be best to wait until morning. There could be little point in waking the household now. Surely, whoever had done this was long gone.

She knew it was her own cowardliness that prompted her reasoning but could not help shrinking at the thought of facing the household. She glanced at Snelling again. If she just left him here, pretended that she had never come belowstairs, . . . he would be found in the morning, and perhaps no one ever need know of her involvement.

Juliana knew the chance was slim, but it was the only hope she had. Grimacing with distaste, she tugged Snelling's greatcoat away from his body and reached into his pocket. She had to be certain that he carried nothing that would indicate he had come to Blandings in search of her.

Five minutes later, she rose to her feet, relieved that Snelling had no papers on him. She glanced at the tall window still standing ajar, then decided it would be best to leave everything just as she had found it. She carefully replaced the candelabrum in its customary place and, after lighting the single taper she'd brought down, extinguished the rest of the candles.

Juliana did not fall asleep until close to four in the morning, and even then she rested only fitfully, tormented by dreams of Snelling and Lucian, of darkness and shadows, and the memory of the black basalt statue.

She awoke in a damp sweat at eight but felt too tired to rise and too troubled to try to sleep again. She sat up in bed, mercilessly reliving the events of the night. In the clear light of morning, she knew she should have summoned Oliver the instant she found Snelling. Now, if it came out that Juliana knew the runner, that it was she he had come to meet, it would look so much worse for her. Who would believe in her innocence?

At nine the maid came in with Juliana's morning chocolate, which she drank thankfully, savoring the small warmth it provided. It was only after Margie had left that Juliana realized Snelling had obviously not been found. The maid had chattered about the pretty morning and how the rain had cleared the air, but not a word about a strange man found in the library.

It was odd, for the maids always tidied the rooms early and placed fresh flowers in the drawing rooms and the library. Mrs. Throckmorton insisted on it. Perhaps they had not done the library yet, Juliana thought, and felt a moment's remorse for the shock Emily or Margie would suffer.

The discovery could not be delayed much longer. Reluctantly she rose and hurriedly dressed, then went down to the breakfast parlor. Bright sunlight streamed in the open window, and she noticed at once the fresh flowers on the table—deep red roses that grew in the terrace garden just beyond the library.

"Good morning, my dear," Mrs. Throckmorton greeted her pleasantly. "May I pour you a cup of tea?"

Juliana nodded mutely and took her customary place. Neither Melody nor Damaris had come down yet, but Faustus lolled beneath the table. She accepted the cup her employer handed her, nudged the dog aside, and managed to inquire if Mrs. Throckmorton had slept well.

"Oh, yes. I always do when it storms, you know. I find the sound of rain beating against the windows somehow comforting. I suppose 'tis because we are safe and warm inside. Do you not find it so?"

"I am afraid not. The noise keeps me awake and I tend to imagine that I hear strange sounds in the house."

"I find that most interesting. My cousin is just the same, but she has a rather nervous disposition, which certainly you do not. Of course, Mavis was badly frightened once when a tree fell on the house—," she broke off to speak to her daughter and niece as they came into the parlor together.

Melody kissed her mother, bid Juliana a cheerful good morning, and took her seat. Damaris, still sulky, sat down opposite and demanded, "Where is Oliver? I particularly wished to ride with him this morning."

"Then you must come down earlier, my dear," her aunt replied. "He went out an hour ago. Do you wish tea or chocolate?"

Juliana allowed the conversation to flow around her.

She swallowed a piece of buttered toast, though she had no appetite, and tried to concentrate on what the others were saying. She sat tensely, expecting to hear a startled scream at any moment from one of the maids.

"You will go with me, will you not, Miss Spencer?" Damaris asked.

Juliana stared at her blankly. "I beg your pardon. My mind was wandering. Go with you where?"

Damaris sighed noisily. "No one ever listens to me. I *must* go into Chichester. I just explained. Oliver was to go with me, but now he has disappeared and I really must purchase some new ribbons."

"I suppose so," Juliana said. "Provided your aunt has no objection."

"Indeed, no. If you are going into town, I have one or two commissions you might perform for me."

Juliana agreed, but she was certain no one would be leaving the house. Yet when another twenty minutes had passed without anyone discovering the body, she began to wonder if she had not imagined the entire incident. A terrible nightmare ... The thought was comforting, but she knew it had been all too real. Unable to bear the suspense any longer, she begged to be excused.

"But I am ready to go," Damaris protested.

"I shall join you in the courtyard in ten minutes," Juliana promised. "I left a book in the library that must be returned to town."

"Oh, botheration. I hope you do not intend to waste the entire morning in Pritchard's."

Ignoring her, Juliana hurried along to the library. This morning all the doors stood ajar and the long hall was flooded with sunlight. It looked so innocent, so peaceful, it was difficult to believe it was the same frightening corridor she'd crept down the night before.

Fearfully, Juliana glanced into the library.

The tall windows were open to catch the morning

breeze. A large bouquet of flowers graced the center table, and, on the pedestal, the black basalt statue reposed just as it always had. The room looked entirely, blessedly normal.

Except that Snelling's body had disappeared.

Chapter 7

Juliana flinched when the maid came up behind her.

"Excuse me, Miss Spencer, I didn't mean to startle you, but Miss Montague is waiting out front and sent me to see what is keeping you."

"I shall be out directly—Margie, who cleaned the library this morning?"

"I did, miss. Is something wrong?"

"No . . . but . . . I was just wondering if you noticed anything out of the ordinary?"

The maid shot a dark look toward the door. "Did Mr. Wilfred complain, miss? I told him it weren't me or Emily that left the windows unlatched last night. We went up to bed together and didn't come down till we was roused this morning. If anyone is slipping out at night, more like it's one of the footmen. Henry Conners, I'd say."

"No one said anything, Margie. 'Tis only that I left something in here last night and now it seems to have disappeared."

"What was it, miss? Shall I help you look?"

Just a dead body. Juliana imagined the maid's shock were she to tell her the truth. Aloud she said, "I seemed to have mislaid a book, but 'tis not important. I shall look again later—"

"Miss Spencer, are you coming?" Damaris demanded from the doorway.

"Yes, dear," Juliana replied absently. She cast one last glance over her shoulder as she left the room. She had not just dreamed of meeting Snelling last night. He had been here, in this room, she was certain of that much. But someone had moved the body.

The murderer?

In a daze, Juliana hurried out to the waiting carriage. Fortunately, Damaris was still sulking, and conversation was not required during the brief drive into Chichester. Mrs. Throckmorton's books were duly exchanged at Pritchard's Lending Library for the latest novels.

"I don't know why Aunt Caroline bothers," Damaris muttered as they left the shop. "It is not as though she *reads* the books."

Juliana usually chastised her charge for such remarks, which she inevitably made every time they visited Pritchard's. It was true that Mrs. Throckmorton was not a reader—Juliana could not recall ever seeing her employer so much as open a book—but she was a considerate hostess, and she liked to have the latest novels at hand for her guests. Damaris took the less charitable view that her aunt only wanted the books, ostentatiously displayed in the drawing room, to impress others.

Today, however, Juliana remained silent, too preoccupied with her own thoughts to pay heed to her companion. She consulted her list and directed Damaris to various merchants, purchasing several pounds of tea, salt, and rice before finally calling at the confectionery shop for the bonbons Mrs. Throckmorton dearly loved. Then they were free to visit the mercer's in St. Martin's Square, where Mrs. Lambert provided an abundant assortment of rich brocades, bright silks, colorful ribbons, brilliantly dyed feathers, and other accoutrements necessary to a lady's wardrobe.

Had she been more observant, Juliana might have noticed that Damaris showed little interest in the lavish displays. For all her urgent declarations that she simply must purchase a new ribbon for her straw hat, she appeared far more concerned with the parade of persons passing in front of the shop windows. They had been in the mercer's less than five minutes when Damaris suddenly picked up a handful of silk ribbons, remarking that she had found just the thing.

After paying for her purchases, they stepped outside—just in time to encounter Mr. Marling as he strolled toward the shop.

"Why, Miss Spencer and Miss Montague. This is a most pleasant surprise."

"Is it?" Juliana murmured. "I rather thought such a meeting preordained."

"I am sure I do not know what you can mean," he replied easily, his thin lips twisted into a smile while his hazel eyes mocked her. "But I am never one to question good fortune."

"Oh, pay no heed to Miss Spencer," Damaris said. "She is always quoting books and such that no one understands. Will you not walk with us to our carriage?"

"It would give me the greatest pleasure," he replied. "Allow me to carry that parcel for you."

Damaris handed him her ribbons and said with an elaborate show of indifference, "Do tell me, Mr. Marling, have you seen Miss Milhouse of late? I had hoped to call on her yesterday, but the rain kept us at home. Such a dreadfully dreary day."

"A pity, then, that you did not venture out. Fitzhugh and I paid Miss Milhouse a visit and spent a most agreeable afternoon. Have you seen her new Bagatelle Board? No? 'Tis an amusing way to pass a few hours. I do wish you might have joined us."

"It appears you had a pleasant enough time without my company," Damaris replied, and there was no mistaking the annoyance in her voice.

"Ah, but your presence would have chased away the storm clouds and brought the sun out, which would have been a vast improvement, I can tell you. That inept driver of mine misjudged the road in the storm last night and nearly overturned the carriage. As it was, we lost a wheel, which kept me from keeping a rather important engagement."

Mollified, Damaris smiled up at him. "Why thank you, Mr. Marling. 'Tis kind of you to say so, and I am distressed to hear about your carriage. I trust you had it mended?" When he nodded, she added, "If you should see dear Miss Milhouse today, pray tell her that I missed her, but I shall hope very much to see her after church on the morrow."

Juliana had listened with growing impatience to the conversation, and as they turned the corner she greeted the sight of Paxton standing by the landau with welcome relief. She civilly thanked Marling for his escort, maneuvered Damaris into the carriage, then left the gentleman standing in the road.

Worried by her own affairs, and annoyed with both Marling and Damaris, Juliana barely waited until the carriage started rolling before she said, "Good heavens, Damaris, how can you abide that popinjay?"

"If you are referring to Mr. Marling, I think he is a charming gentleman. Just because he does not trouble to flatter you—"

"He does not flatter me because he knows well enough that I would never believe the sort of balderdash he spouts, and I must say I am surprised that you do. I have always thought you an intelligent girl, but it is obvious that when it comes to Marling, your wits have gone begging. However, if you think your aunt, or your uncle, will ever countenance a match with him, you are very much mistaken."

"I suppose I am to have no say in whom I wed?"

"Not if you show such poor judgment as to arrange a tryst with someone like Marling. Really, Damaris, it is patently obvious that you were to meet him at Miss Milhouse's yesterday, and if that were not possible, at the mercer's today. Your aunt would be extremely vexed if she knew your urgent need to purchase ribbons was a mere pretext to meet Marling."

"You are imagining things," Damaris protested, but her blush betrayed her. She stared mulishly out the window, then, a moment later, asked softly, "You will not tell Aunt Caroline, will you?"

"I should," Juliana said. "However, I will refrain for now if you give me your word that you will not arrange any further meetings with Marling. Damaris, my dear, I only want you to be happy. Marling is a gazetted fortune hunter. If he truly cared for you, he would not ask you to meet him in this manner."

When Damaris did not reply, Juliana deemed it wisest to say nothing more. Her head ached unbearably and she longed for the solitude of her own bedchamber to puzzle out the mysterious disappearance of Snelling's body.

Lord Dysart bided his time, dutifully laughing as his hostess related a delicious bon mot about an extremely well-connected gentlemen in London, caught in a most embarrassing position when the rather disreputable house he was visiting suddenly caught fire. Dysart stretched out his booted legs, encouraged Mrs. Throckmorton with a question, and to all appearances seemed utterly content. Inside, he seethed.

Where the devil was Miss Spencer? After contriving to meet young Throckmorton and wangling an invitation to return to Blandings for a cup of tea, Dysart's plans had gone sadly awry. Miss Spencer, whom he had pictured as pacing the floor and near frantic with worry, was not at home. She, he learned, had gone shopping with Miss Montague.

He knew his annoyance was irrational. The lady could have no way of knowing that he intended to call today to set her mind at ease. And certainly she would have to continue with her duties, but it was annoying all the same. He smiled at Mrs. Throckmorton and accepted a second cup of tea while avoiding his secretary's glance of surprise.

His patience was rewarded some moments later when Mrs. Throckmorton glanced toward the door and called out, "Oh, do come in, Miss Spencer. Damaris, my dear, is it not fortunate you returned just now? I know you would not like to have missed his lordship and Mr. Harrington."

The gentlemen rose to their feet as the ladies entered the room. Dysart relieved Miss Spencer of the armful of books she carried and, after a flurry of greetings were exchanged, relinquished his seat near the tea table to her. He remained standing, positioning himself near the fireplace so that he could covertly observe her expressions.

Oliver, wondering at his lordship's willingness to stay tamely drinking tea and gossiping, begged leave to be excused. Charles, however, seemed content to remain and seated himself on the sofa beside Miss Montague, immediately engaging her in conversation.

"Do sit down, Lord Dysart," Mrs. Throckmorton coaxed as she prepared a cup of tea for Juliana.

"Thank you, but I should like to stand for awhile. I find one becomes rather stiff after riding if one sits too long. Indeed, I am hoping to persuade Miss Montague and Miss Spencer to take a turn about the garden. After they have their tea, of course."

"Where is Melody?" Juliana asked. "She usually takes Faustus for a walk in the afternoon."

"She is visiting the vicarage, my dear. Poor Pamela has been ordered to bed—measles, you know. She is in an agony of embarrassment at breaking out in spots, and Mrs. Trilby thought a visit from Melody might cheer her."

"Measles! Good heavens, I hope she is not contagious," Damaris cried. "How dreadful to come out in spots at her age."

"Very lowering," Mrs. Throckmorton agreed. "But Melody had measles when she was four, or maybe five . . . and Oliver, I distinctly remember, had them when he was very small. Terribly ill he was, and too little to understand why he was so sick. Still, I am thankful they had them when they were young. Best to get it over with, and Dr. Girard told me 'tis most unlikely they will ever get them again. Damaris, my dear, do you recall having measles?"

She shook her head. "I do not remember. . . ."

"Well, I shall write to your uncle and inquire, and to your Aunt Margaret, too, but it is doubtful that we shall hear soon—the mail is so slow these days. Still, I cannot help but think that it would be best if you refrained from visiting the vicarage until Pamela is quite recovered."

Damaris, who had not the slightest intention of doing anything so foolish, nodded mutely.

"And you, Miss Spencer?" Dysart asked. "Have you had measles?"

She nodded, "A gift from my brother. We were both ill at the same time, and I can recall that he made a game of it. We used to count our spots to see who had the most. However, I suspect he cheated."

"That is utterly disgusting," Damaris declared.

Dysart laughed, but a vague memory plagued him. He had heard a similar story once. . . . He'd been at school and several boys were quarantined. . . .

Damaris jumped up. "I cannot abide any more talk of illness and such. Let us take a walk through the garden."

Charles rose obediently and offered his arm, while Lord Dysart looked inquiringly at Juliana.

She wanted only to be alone, but duty required that she accompany her young charge. Managing a smile, she rose. "That sounds most pleasant."

They spoke of the weather, which had cleared the air and produced a balmy afternoon, and of the assembly in Chichester on Wednesday evening. Damaris chattered breathlessly. She easily dominated the conversation, her words running together like raindrops in a lake. Miss Spencer said little.

Dysart halted near one of the rosebushes and, under the pretext of admiring the flowers, waited until Charles and Damaris had strolled some distance ahead. Then he remarked casually, "Have you heard the latest rumor going around? My secretary told me there is a Bow Street Runner putting up at the Rose and Crown. One wonders what brings him to Chichester."

"Perhaps he is just . . . just visiting," she replied as she broke off a wilted flower.

"I suppose that is always possible, but Charles said the man was asking a lot of questions about a young lady. Oddly enough, she seems to bear some resemblance to you."

"Does she? That is odd," she murmured, carefully avoiding his eyes.

Dysart watched her for a moment, wishing he could ease the constraint he heard in her voice. She would not look at him, but the flower trembling in her hand and the stiff way she held her shoulders caused a wrenching ache in his heart. He said gently, "The man seems to have disappeared, but the trouble with runners is that when one leaves another takes his place. I should like to help you, my dear, but I cannot do so unless you confide in me."

"I do not know what you mean, sir," she said, moving away from him.

Dysart came up behind her. "There is no need for you to dissemble, Miss Spencer. I saw you in the library last night."

"You saw me?" she asked, whirling to face him. Her eyes mirrored her confusion—and her anger. "Were you spying on me, my lord?"

"I would not call it spying, Miss Spencer. You see, I chanced, quite by accident, to overhear part of your conversation with Snelling last Friday. I had stepped out on the terrace for a smoke and saw him enter the library in a rather furtive manner. Naturally, I wanted to be certain that he was not a burglar."

"I see, and you heard his demand for fifty pounds? Is that why you were so helpful in pawning my jewels?"

He nodded. "I would have given you the money gladly or sent Snelling on his way, had you given me leave. But you seemed determined to conduct this business yourself, and all I could do was be at hand in case you had need of my help. Fortuitously, it seems, in light of what occurred."

"I suppose I should thank you, my lord, but your interference has made a troublesome situation a great deal more difficult. I do not mean to sound unappreciative, but was it necessary to hit Mr. Snelling quite so hard?"

"Hit him?" Dysart repeated, staring at her incredulously. "I did not lay a glove on him—at least not until he was already stretched out on your library floor. Thanks to the storm, I was a few moments late arriving. When I came up on the terrace, I saw you kneeling beside the body. I assumed he must have threatened you, refused the money, or demanded more—"

"And you thought for such a reason I would bash him over the head? Really, my lord, you have a very low opinion of my character."

104

"And you of mine," he retorted. "Obviously, you had no trouble imagining I had murdered someone."

She had the grace to blush. "I believed that, in a misguided effort to protect me, you might have hit him, perhaps harder than you intended."

"Well, I didn't," Dysart swore. "And that leaves us with a very interesting question, Miss Spencer. If you did not bash him, and I certainly did not, then who did? Did you tell anyone that you were meeting this man?"

Juliana shook her head. "Hardly, my lord. It is not the sort of thing one mentions in polite conversation . . . but I do not understand what happened to Snelling. Someone moved his body and—"

"I did," Dysart interrupted.

"You? But why?"

"Is it not obvious, Miss Spencer? I thought you had taken fright and hit him over the head. I was trying to protect you."

"Well, I wish you had not," she replied ungraciously. Then, curiously, "What did you do with . . . with the body?"

"He's buried in the rose garden, about a dozen paces beyond the sundial."

"Good heavens," she cried, feeling faint as her eyes darted to the path just a few feet away. "Was that the best you could contrive?"

"May I remind you that it was dark, Miss Spencer," he said, his brows drawing together in annoyance. "Not to mention raining hard, and, I might add, Snelling was an exceedingly heavy man. I thought that under the circumstances I managed extremely well."

"Yes, yes, of course, my lord. I just . . . I was thinking of the gardeners."

"I did not intend it as a final resting place. You must realize that if Snelling found you, others will, too. You told him you were innocent of charges made against you. What we must do now is prove your innocence—and as quickly as possible. You must tell me—oh, blast," he muttered as he spotted Charles approaching with Miss Montague. "We cannot discuss this now. Ride out with me tomorrow. I shall call for you at one."

"I cannot, my lord. To be seen riding with you would give rise to the worst sort of gossip. You must realize that a lady in my position must be extremely careful not to—"

"Your position is already extremely awkward, my dear," Dysart interrupted. "But never mind. Meet me here at midnight. We shall talk then."

"My lord, I—"

"Midnight," he whispered insistently. "Now, smile." He turned her to face Charles and Miss Montague and, for their benefit, added loudly, "London is not what it used to be. Particularly during the Season."

Damaris eyed them suspiciously. "What were you discussing a moment ago, my lord? I remarked to Mr. Harrington that I had never seen you look so angry."

Dysart appeared puzzled for a moment, then laughed. "That must have been when I was ranting about my tailor. You would not credit the absolutely horrid waistcoat the fellow sent down. Don't get me started, Miss Montague. Every time I think of it, my blood boils. And the worst of it is, I'd planned to wear the thing to the Assembly Rooms on Wednesday. Now I fear I shall have to send Charles up to Town."

"But a waistcoat?" Charles admonished as he sat in the library at Windward with his employer that evening. He glanced regretfully at the brandy decanter that he had emptied as he listened with growing incredulity to his lordship's confidences. That Miss Spencer was being blackmailed was difficult enough to credit; that this despicable person was now dead and buried by Lord Dysart in the rose garden stretched taut the bounds of belief. But asking one to accept that his lordship's tailor, the superb Weston, had sent down a garish waistcoat, was going too far. The notion was ridiculous. Why, even to consider it made his head ache.

Aloud he said, "I fear you give Miss Montague too little credit. Her understanding is such that I doubt she will be bamboozled by such a tale."

"It was the best I could think of at the moment," Dysart replied, a trifle annoyed. "Obviously, I have not the creative powers I once supposed. Miss Spencer was less than pleased that I disposed of Snelling in the rose garden."

"Perhaps it was not the . . . the wisest choice," Charles remarked, his words slurring slightly. When Dysart glared at him, he added hastily, "But I quite understand your . . . your, uh, dilemma."

"The man weighed closed to fourteen stone. What would you have done?"

"Retreated."

"Nonsense. You know you would not have left a lady in such a predicament. No gentleman would."

Charles sighed, then downed what little brandy remained in his glass. "Difficult . . . very difficult, my lord, but I doubt my father would approve." He considered the matter further, then shook his head. "No, I am very certain Father would advise one not to move the body. Snelling is bound to be missed, you know."

Dysart rose and paced restlessly. "Of course, which is why we must act quickly. First Miss Spencer must be cleared of the charges leveled against her, and then we must discover who is responsible for Snelling's untimely demise."

"Must we, sir?" Charles asked, wishing his lordship would stand still. "It seems to me that Mr. Snelling was less than an . . . an admirable person. He was perse . . . pressa . . . persecuting Miss Spencer. We don't want that sort around. Let sleeping dogs lie. Or in this case, runners," Charles said, ending his words on a hiccup.

Dysart glanced at his secretary. The man's eyes were unfocused, his words had become slurred, and the brandy glass waved unsteadily in the air. It was the first time he'd ever seen his impeccable secretary under the hatches. He grinned. "Go to bed, Charles."

"I shall . . . wait for . . . you, my lord . . . ," his secretary mumbled as his head lolled slowly backward. His eyes drifted shut and, a moment later, a loud snore waffled past his lips.

Charles would be mortified in the morning, the earl thought as he pulled the bellrope. Barely a moment later, a discreet tap sounded on the door, and a footman stepped into the room. Dysart motioned toward his secretary. "Please assist Mr. Harrington to his bed, George, and tell Roberts not to wait up for me. I shall be going out shortly."

"Yes, my lord," the footman replied. Well-trained, he showed not the slightest surprise as he struggled to get Mr. Harrington on his feet and to the hall. It was not an easy task.

After closing the door behind the stumbling pair, Dysart strode to his desk and lit a cigar. Now he allowed the memories that had plagued him all day full rein. Miss Spencer did not realize it, but she had given him a clue to her identity that afternoon.

Dysart recalled Philip deVere, the closest friend he'd had at Oxford. They had been inseparable from the start, finding in each other a kindred spirit. Philip, always ready to run any rig, loyal to the nth degree. Philip, who'd talked incessantly about his family and his pretty little sister, Lady Juliana. It had all come back to Dysart this afternoon when Miss Spencer mentioned having had measles. Philip had told him the same tale. Confined to the nursery with his sister, the pair of them had nothing to do, and he had finally made a contest of seeing who had the most spots.

He realized now that Miss Spencer had reminded him of Philip from the first. She had the same coloring, the same way of speaking certain words, the same little mannerisms. He had been a fool not to spot the resemblance sooner.

Only one hardly expected Lady Juliana, the beloved daughter of the wealthy Duke of Sunderland, to be employed as a companion. Even had her father fallen on hard times—and surely Dysart would have heard if such was the case—Philip would have looked after his sister. He'd been devoted to her.

Dysart racked his brains, trying to recall the last time he'd heard from his old friend. Could it really be almost three years? After they had left Oxford, Philip had written occasionally, always inviting Dysart to visit Morcombe, but there had never been sufficient time. Of course, he'd suggested his friend come to London instead . . . they had even set a date once, but then Philip's mother had died, and their plans were canceled. Dysart had sent his condolences, but he couldn't recall hearing from his friend since.

Three years. Guilt bit at his conscience. Philip deVere had his share of pride, and if he had suffered financial reverses, he was not the sort to presume on an old friendship. His silence should have alerted Dysart that something was dreadfully amiss. Shaking his head, he silently swore that when this business was finished, he would drive to Morcombe himself. Even if his suspicions were wrong, and Miss Spencer was not the lady he thought her, he would still seek out Philip and renew their friendship.

Dysart drew out his watch. Half past eleven. He

dearly hoped Miss Spencer would keep their tryst. He had several questions he wished to ask that young lady. And if she should continue to prove reticent, he would send Charles to Morcombe on the morrow to find out the truth.

Chapter 8

Lord Dysart rose from the garden bench when he saw Miss Spencer cautiously step out of the library. "Over here," he called softly.

Her eyes slowly becoming adjusted to the pale moonlight, Juliana waved a hand to signal that she had seen him, then hurriedly crossed the terrace to where he waited. "I really should not be here, my lord."

His brows arched upward. "I see. You are quite willing to meet a runner who wanted to blackmail you, but it goes against your scruples to keep an engagement with a gentleman who wishes only to be of assistance."

Despite the hour and the gravity of her situation, Juliana nearly smiled. "How foolish that sounds, but you must know that I was not at all willing to meet Mr. Snelling. I simply had no choice."

"And I have given you none either," he said ruefully.

She glanced up at him, thinking how devilishly handsome he looked in the moonlight . . . and in the morning light, and at every other hour she had seen him. It was patently unfair that any gentleman should possess both charm and good looks in such abundance. Reining in her wayward thoughts, she said, "The cases are hardly similar, my lord. I acquit you of all but the purest motives, although why you should involve yourself in my affairs puzzles me."

"Does it? Perhaps 'tis only because you seem to have

111

no one else to help you. Have you no family, Miss Spencer?"

"No . . . no one but a cousin whom I cannot abide."

"You mentioned a brother—"

"He died some time ago," she interrupted curtly, then sighed. "I apologize for my rudeness, my lord. I know you mean only to help, but I still find it painful to speak of my brother's death."

Dysart hesitated. She did not appear to be dissembling. Had he been wrong after all? Surely someone would have thought to notify him had Philip died unexpectedly. And yet, as he gazed at her, he could swear there was a strong resemblance to his old friend.

Juliana glanced nervously toward the house. "My lord, if we are discovered together, the scandal will be such that even your mother will hear of it in France."

He laughed. "I assure you, Miss Spencer, I am no stranger to scandal, and Maman does not listen to gossip—fortunately. But for all that, you are right. We should not dally longer than necessary. Tell me quickly about this business with Snelling. What brought him here?"

Juliana blushed. Turning slightly away from him, she replied in a dull voice, "When I left my cousin's protection, he set it about that I . . . I had stolen a priceless necklace—it is known as the Sunderland Diamonds and has been in our family for generations. He knows that I did not, my lord, but he uses that as an excuse to employ men to find me. Mr. Snelling told me that Lucian seemed far more interested in locating me than in recovering the diamonds."

"Please understand that I am not doubting you, but such action seems somewhat extreme. What could your cousin hope to gain?"

Her blush deepened. "He is an extremely proud man, my lord, and also a vindictive one. After my brother died,

Lucian . . . proposed to me. When I refused his offer, he swore I would wed him or no one." When Dysart remained silent, she turned to steal a look at him. He was studying her pensively. Did he doubt her? Was he already regretting his offer of assistance?

She plucked at the fringe of the shawl she'd draped about her shoulders. "I know this must sound rather melodramatic, but you do not know my cousin. He cannot bear to be crossed, and those who do so usually regret it greatly. A friend, who defied Lucian and offered me shelter for a few days, came home to find his stables in flames. Another gentleman who bested my cousin in a horse race found his prized stallion's foreleg brutally slashed open the following day. Of course nothing could be proved, but I can recount dozens of other such incidents."

"Are you trying to warn me off, Miss Spencer?"

"No, but perhaps I should. Every person who has befriended me has suffered in some way. And I must tell you, my lord, that it would not surprise me to learn that my cousin is behind Mr. Snelling's death. Indeed, I have been giving this some thought. Lucian employed this runner, and if he somehow managed to follow him here . . ." She broke off, shivering as she thought of her cousin's vile temper.

"I think you are letting your fear of this man frighten you unnecessarily. Only consider, Snelling would scarce have had time to have written anyone. And why would he have done so? You said yourself that he wanted nothing more to do with your cousin."

She shrugged. "That is what the runner told me, my lord, but perhaps he planned all along to notify Lucian, or had already done so. Snelling would have my fifty pounds, and whatever else my cousin was paying him as well."

"I suppose that's possible, but if that were so, then

113

what reason could your cousin have for killing his own man?"

She swung around to face him, her eyes glistening a deep blue-green in the moonlight. "He might do so merely to implicate me. . . . I would set nothing beyond him," she replied, her voice rife with loathing. "And what other explanation could there be? No one here would have reason to do away with Snelling."

"We don't know that," Dysart said, seeking to ease some of her anxiety. "Snelling was a runner. Is it not possible that he chanced upon you while investigating some other person?"

"In Chichester?" Her brows lifted at the absurdity. "There are no strangers in the area, except for Mr. Marling."

"Aha," Dysart pounced. "It is generally believed that Marling abandoned London in order to pursue Miss Montague, but perhaps he had another reason for abruptly leaving Town."

"I hardly think—," Juliana began, but broke off as she heard a noise. It sounded like a boot scraping on the terrace.

"Stay here," Dysart whispered as his keen eyes searched the area. He thought he'd heard someone near the library. Moving as quietly as his Wellingtons would permit, he strode toward the tall windows. His eyes had long since adjusted to the dim moonlight, and he caught a flash of movement in the shrubbery. Giving up any effort to be quiet, he dashed toward the railing, preparing to vault over it, but was brought up short.

"What the devil?" he cursed as a soft hand suddenly clutched at his arm.

"Lord Dysart, is that you? La, sir, you gave me a horrible fright. I quite thought you were a burglar."

"Damaris! What are you doing out here at this hour?" Juliana demanded, coming up behind the earl.

"I might ask you the same," the girl retorted as she glanced from Lord Dysart to her companion. "But it appears the answer is obvious."

"You are mistaken, but my conduct is not in question," Juliana replied, though she could not help the blush that tinged her cheeks. "I want to know what you are doing out here at this hour, and you will answer me immediately or I shall summon your aunt."

"If you must know, I thought I heard someone on the terrace," Damaris said sulkily. "My room is above the library, and an odd noise awoke me. Of course, I realize now it must have been you and his lordship. How sly you are, Miss Spencer. I am sure my aunt will be most interested to know—"

"Your aunt will not hear a word of this," Dysart interrupted, his voice pleasantly low but threatening all the same. "Or I shall tell Lady Throckmorton *you* were meeting someone, and I would have caught the person had you not deliberately prevented me. Who was it, Miss Montague? Marling?"

"You are quite mad, my lord," Damaris said as she edged toward the house. "But if you want to have a tryst with Miss Spencer, I am sure it is no concern of mine." As she was about to step inside the house, she added impudently, "Only I do hope you will try to be more quiet. I really do need my sleep."

Dysart would have laughed aloud at the girl's audaciousness, but it was clear Miss Spencer was considerably upset. He advised her, "Pay the little vixen no heed. She is too worried about her own situation to speak of this. I'll wager any amount you like that it was Marling she was meeting."

"Yes, I fear 'tis so, and Damaris is too young to realize the risk she is running. Marling could ruin her. I should alert Mrs. Throckmorton. Perhaps we could—"

"Forget Miss Montague," Dysart interrupted impa-

115

tiently. "She would only deny it, and judging from what I've seen of her, Mrs. Throckmorton would not pursue the matter."

"But I cannot just stand by and allow Damaris to meet Marling—suppose she elopes with him?"

"It would serve her right."

"You may find this a matter for jest, my lord, but it is my responsibility to see she comes to no harm. Mrs. Throckmorton pays me most generously, and I would be grievously remiss in my duty were I to do nothing."

"I keep forgetting your lamentable regard for duty," Dysart muttered. "However, if it will relieve your mind, I will have a word with Marling in the morning and warn him off."

Her eyes glowed with appreciation, and she said softly, "Thank you, my lord. I know you think the matter trifling—"

"At the moment, I do. You stand in a great deal more danger than Miss Montague. Our first priority must be to clear your name."

"You are very kind, but what you are suggesting is impossible. My cousin is a powerful man, and I have no proof of my suspicions. Were I to come forward, it would be his word against mine."

"You must at least try," he urged gently. "You cannot stay in hiding forever."

Juliana sighed. "I have done so for two years, my lord, and 'tis better than confronting Lucian. He would find some way to . . . to implicate me. I dare not provoke him further."

"But if, as you suspect, he is here, what will you do then?"

Her shoulders drooping at the prospect before her, Juliana whispered, "Disappear again. Eventually, he will tire of searching for me."

The thought unnerved Dysart. He had a sudden vision

116

of calling at Blandings one day only to learn that Miss Spencer had mysteriously vanished during the night. He reached out and tucked her cold hands in his, drawing her close. "Promise me you will do nothing rash."

For a few brief seconds, Juliana basked in the knowledge that she was not quite alone in the world, that Lord Dysart cared enough to be concerned . . . but then she recalled her situation and reluctantly tried to withdraw her hands. "I must go in, my lord."

"Your promise first," he insisted, refusing to let her go.

"I promise I shall do nothing tonight but seek my bed and think what I shall say to Damaris on the morrow."

He was not entirely satisfied, but he let her go. "Try not to worry, my dear. I shall think of some way to help you, I give you my word."

She nodded, but once safely inside, she scolded herself severely for her foolishness. It was not her scruples, as Lord Dysart believed, that had made her hesitate to meet him, but her own growing attachment for the gentleman. Foolish, indeed, she thought as she climbed the stairs to her bedchamber, when anyone could see that his lordship merely felt sorry for her. Even if he should come to feel more strongly, she knew she had no future with him—or with any other gentleman—until she could reveal her true identity. And that remained an impossibility.

As she was about to step inside her room, she heard the sound of a door closing softly. Damaris! Spying on me, Juliana thought. She hesitated a moment, wondering if it wouldn't be better to talk to the girl at once, to try to explain . . . but what, after all, could she say? Too weary to think clearly, Juliana closed the door to her own room and uttered a brief prayer that somehow things would look different on the morrow.

Sunday dawned gray and overcast, matching Juliana's downcast spirits. Neither the weather nor her mood improved as the day progressed. Damaris had been impossible, casting sly hints and innuendos at every opportunity. And to make matters worse, this was the fourth Sunday of the month, which meant the party from Blandings would take dinner at the vicarage.

The custom was of some duration, but the meal was never a happy one, for Mrs. Trilby had no notion of how to set a table. She was an inept hostess, and no matter how hard she tried, her dinners were either overcooked or underdone. Of course, she had not Mrs. Throckmorton's chef or extensive staff to assist her, so her meals were served *à la française*, which presented several difficulties. The dishes were left on the table in such a manner as to be invariably cooled before they were sampled and those gentlemen accustomed to being served by a footman found themselves at a loss when faced with a fowl or roast and a carving knife. More than one bird had slipped off the plate into some luckless gentleman's lap.

Mrs. Throckmorton had confided to Miss Spencer after such an incident, "One wonders that dear Mrs. Trilby does not think to have the meat carved before 'tis carried to the table, but there—she is so very nice and means so well, one cannot possibly complain."

Of course one could and did—particularly Damaris, who turned up her tiny nose at the cold asparagus and peas, and declared the roast saddle of mutton dry as a bone and the venison nearly raw. She made no pretense of eating and whispered her criticism to Oliver, seated next to her, who bluntly told her she had no manners and would have done better to remain at home. Their low-voice conversation quickly evolved into a loud squabble, much to everyone's embarrassment, and Mrs. Trilby hastily signaled that it was time the ladies retired.

Conversation in the drawing room was stilted. Damaris, aware she had gone beyond the line, withdrew to an alcove with Pamela, Melody, and Charlotte Chadleigh, leaving the older ladies to talk among themselves.

Mrs. Throckmorton, embarrassed by her niece's behavior, keenly felt the pitying glances cast in her direction by Mrs. Fitzhugh and Mrs. Chadleigh. Trying to make light of the incident, she remarked, "Dear Damaris and Oliver are so like brother and sister, one cannot leave them together for more than a few moments or they are arguing. Of course, it means nothing."

Mrs. Fitzhugh reached across and patted her hand. "My dear Caroline, one can only sympathize. So good of you to take the child in, but we all realize Miss Montague must be a sad trial to you."

Mrs. Throckmorton fumed silently. She loathed being patronized by Emily Fitzhugh, and however much she might deplore Damaris's lack of manners, she would never admit it to the world at large. Managing a laugh, Caroline replied, "A trial? Good heavens, no. Damaris has a . . . a very kind heart. Of course, she has not had the advantages of Melody or dear Pamela, but anyone who knows her well cannot help but be fond of her."

"Certainly a number of gentlemen are," Mrs. Fitzhugh remarked with a titter. "I hear Mr. Marling is quite smitten."

Juliana, sitting slightly withdrawn as she felt befitted her position, glanced at the lady sharply.

"That is *not* a connection we wish to encourage," Mrs. Throckmorton said firmly.

Mrs. Fitzhugh allowed a small smile to cross her lips. "You may not, but perhaps Miss Montague entertains other ideas. She certainly seems to welcome his attention. I saw her strolling with him in the village just yesterday, and if that is her notion of discouraging a gentleman, well all I can say is that it's certainly not mine."

Juliana very uncharitably wished the woman at the devil, but she smiled pleasantly and said, "Perhaps Miss

Montague finds it difficult, as I do, to cut a gentleman who is received in so many of her friends' homes. As it happened, I was with her when we chanced to meet Mr. Marling, and I can tell you that he said nothing one could take exception to, and he most courteously escorted us to our carriage. I doubt we were in his company above ten minutes."

Mrs. Trilby, aware of the tension in her drawing room, sought to turn the conversation and remarked ingenuously, "Well, he seems a nice enough young man—not suitable for Miss Montague, of course—but very pleasant, though I much prefer the company of Lord Dysart. Are we not fortunate to have such a charming gentleman in our midst?"

"Indeed, yes," Mrs. Throckmorton enthused. "He has been much at Blandings. Such condescension, my dears. Not at all high in the instep as one might well expect from a gentleman of his rank."

Emily Fitzhugh plied her fan as she remarked, "I know he is most agreeable, but, my dear, his reputation! Are you sure 'tis wise to allow him to run tame in your house? My son told me his lordship seems to have a marked partiality for a certain young lady at Blandings."

She cast a sly look at Miss Spencer, but Mrs. Throckmorton did not understand her hint and looked at her in a puzzled way. "If you are referring to my niece, I assure you his lordship treats her much as he would a young sister, and my Melody, too. It would please me greatly were it not so, but I cannot say he has a partiality for either."

Juliana, ready to sink with mortification, was determined not to allow Mrs. Fitzhugh the pleasure of seeing her discomfited. She lifted her chin and said gaily, "If Lord Dysart has a partiality for anyone at Blandings, I fear 'tis Faustus—and the feeling is mutual. Melody's dog quite adores his lordship and can barely be controlled whenever he pays us a visit."

"I have not noticed that animal controlled at any time," Mrs. Chadleigh said. "But then I have never approved of dogs in the drawing room."

Juliana sighed with relief as the gentlemen joined the ladies and the conversation turned to more genial topics. The Reverend Mr. Trilby came up for a few moments. He seldom joined his guests after dinner, claiming the press of work prohibited it. But tonight he announced he would shortly be assisted by a new curate, scheduled to arrive the following week, and he hoped they would all do their utmost to make Mr. Evans feel welcome.

Juliana barely listened as the ladies ascertained that the new curate was a bachelor, and, as far as Mr. Trilby knew, not harboring any attachments. She prayed the evening would be of short duration, but Mrs. Trilby seemed determined to draw it out and asked her daughter to play for the company.

Pamela had a sweet voice, and she played skillfully enough, but it was not often she could be persuaded to perform. Tonight, however, she'd promised her mother, and she nervously took her place at the spinet. She chose a hymn that was one of her papa's favorites, and she sang it with a small degree of feeling. It was an adequate performance, but she appeared so shy and uncertain when she finally looked up that everyone applauded enthusiastically.

Most of the young people present gathered around Pamela and were effusive with their praise. Only Damaris, accustomed to being the center of attention at such gatherings, remained seated on the sofa, her pretty mouth twisted into a sullen expression.

Patrick Fitzhugh, who was particularly fond of Pamela, turned to Damaris and remarked, "Did she not perform splendidly, Miss Montague? I vow I have never heard a sweeter voice."

"Very nice," Damaris agreed with a noticeable lack of

enthusiasm. "Of course, it was difficult to hear her—perhaps if she had some training, her voice might carry better." Her own voice carried extremely well, the words falling into one of those sudden pauses in conversation that sometimes happens in a small room.

An immediate silence followed her remarks, then a chorus of voices rushed to fill the void, Oliver's among them, assuring Miss Trilby that she sang like an angel. Oliver left the group surrounding the young lady and maneuvered until he stood behind his cousin. Casually leaning over the sofa, he said, "Only someone mean-spirited and jealous would find fault with Pamela's performance. I know you're a selfish little beast, but I didn't think you were such a cat."

Though Damaris ignored him, his words had not only hurt but, she knew, were deserved. It *was* mean-spirited of her to speak so of Pamela, but she had felt so envious. The others never complimented her so warmly or made such an obvious effort to make her feel special. With the exception of Pamela, Damaris doubted that anyone in the room even liked her. They may have pretended to, but she knew she was accepted only because she was Melody's cousin.

She looked uneasily around the room, noticing that the other young gentlemen present were all gathered about Pamela. Miss Spencer sent Damaris a speaking glance that promised a lengthy scold when they returned home. She had not long to wait.

No one seemed disposed to linger and, after drinking a last cup of tea, the guests took their leave promptly at ten. Nothing was said in the carriage, save the most trivial of remarks, for Paxton was driving, but when they arrived at Blandings, Mrs. Throckmorton called to her niece as she started up the stairs.

"I should like a word with you before you retire, my

dear. When you've put off your things, please come to my room."

Damaris feigned a yawn. "I am dreadfully tired, Aunt Caroline. Can it not wait until morning?"

"I am afraid not, but I shall not keep you long. Miss Spencer, I should like you to join us, please."

Juliana nodded. She had expected such a summons and, after removing her hat and gloves, went along the hall and tapped softly on Mrs. Throckmorton's door. Known as the Chinese room, the walls here were hung with hand-painted paper, and the elegant bed hangings were of finely wrought Chinese silk. Both featured a green leafy design, and when the morning sun lit the long windows, it gave the room the look of a garden. Juliana had been surprised the first time she'd seen the room, for it did not seem at all Mrs. Throckmorton's taste. But she'd learned the chamber was kept precisely the same as when they bought the house, the late Mr. Throckmorton having been fond of it.

This evening, the curtains were drawn across the windows and a fire was lit, adding a bit of coziness to the vastness of the room. Mrs. Throckmorton sat in front of the intricately carved white and gold mantel, staring up at the portrait of her husband, which dominated the south wall. She glanced around as Miss Spencer entered. "Come in, come in. I was just thinking what Mr. Throckmorton would have to say about this evening. Damaris is his niece, you know, and he set considerable store by family."

"Did he know her?" Juliana asked curiously.

"Not to speak of. We saw her once or twice when she was maybe three or four, and as beautiful a child as I ever laid eyes on." Mrs. Throckmorton sighed heavily. "She was so sweet, and doted on by her papa. Perhaps if he had not passed on so young—" She broke off as Damaris stepped into the room.

"You wished to see me, Aunt Caroline?"

"Yes, my dear. Do come in and sit down." She waited until Damaris warily settled herself in a chair opposite, then said gently, "Although it pains me to say so, I must tell you that I was greatly embarrassed by your behavior this evening. I may not have had the advantages of Miss Spencer, or even Mrs. Trilby, but I know enough to behave politely in company. Miss Spencer is of the opinion that it would be best to give you a Season in Town, but if you cannot comport yourself properly here, I shudder to think what you might do in London."

"Just because I did not fawn all over Pamela—"

"You squabbled with Oliver during dinner, a breach of manners I find appalling—"

"He started it!"

Ignoring her, Mrs. Throckmorton continued, "And then you were rude to a young lady who has always spoken well of you. There was not a person in the room who did not think so."

Damaris tossed her head. "I don't care what they think. They are all so dreadfully provincial. None of them has ever been to London or—"

"Hush," Mrs. Throckmorton ordered in a voice Juliana had never heard her use. It shocked Damaris into silence as well.

"I have made every allowance for your lamentable upbringing. I thought that, given time, your association with Melody and Miss Trilby, and the fine example set for you by Miss Spencer, would have some effect. It is regrettably obvious that I was mistaken."

Damaris shot her companion an angry look. "Has Miss Spencer been complaining of me? Well, she is not nearly as perfect as you think. She has set her cap for Lord Dysart and is jealous just because he—"

"If Miss Spencer spoke of you at all, it was only to make excuses for you," her aunt interrupted. "Not an easy task, I know. Now, I believe you need some time to reflect on the value of friendships and the good opinion of others. Therefore, you will not be permitted to leave the house, nor to receive any callers, for a fortnight."

"You cannot do that," Damaris cried angrily as she rose to her feet.

"Indeed I can, and if I do not see a marked improvement in your deportment, I shall write to your uncle and together we will decide what is best for you. That is all. You may bid us a good evening."

Too angry to speak, Damaris turned and flounced out of the room.

"Oh, dear, I do hope I have done the right thing," Mrs. Throckmorton murmured the moment the door closed behind her niece. She slumped in her chair, her brow creased with worry.

Juliana smiled at her. "I am certain you did. Damaris is a difficult girl, and I think you have been remarkably patient with her, but perhaps what she needs most is a firm hand."

"Well, I don't mind telling you, Miss Spencer, I don't like it a bit. It makes me feel ill having to scold her, and I dread the next two weeks. If this doesn't work, I don't know what I shall do. I have been thinking, and perhaps you are right and I should make arrangements to bring her out. A Season would give her thoughts another direction."

Juliana reluctantly agreed. It would mean the end of her own position, for she dared not risk going to London, where she was likely to meet old friends. She rose and suggested, "I think that might be best, but let us see what the next few days bring. Damaris may surprise us."

"Anything is possible, I suppose."

Juliana smiled and said good evening. She had crossed the room and opened the door when Mrs. Throckmorton called to her. She turned and looked back inquiringly.

"Mrs. Chadleigh made several remarks about Lord

Dysart. It did not occur to me at the time, but when she said he was partial to a young lady at Blandings, she was referring to you, was she not?"

Juliana blushed, but words failed her. She gestured helplessly.

"I thought so," Mrs. Throckmorton said, nodding her blond head. "Well, he's a very sensible young man. Good night, my dear."

Chapter 9

Lord Dysart paced the library Monday evening, waiting impatiently for Charles Harrington's return. He'd expected his secretary the day before or, at the very latest, that morning. It should not take so long to drive to Morcombe and back. Striding to the long windows and staring mindlessly at the sweep of lawn, Dysart lit a cigar. He could have made the journey in two days—three at most. But Charles had been gone for five days and time was a luxury they could ill afford.

Dysart cursed silently, wondering once again why he had become entangled in Miss Spencer's affairs. Certainly the lady did not seem to appreciate his efforts on her behalf. She stubbornly refused to make any attempt to clear her name and obstinately insisted that the mysterious Lucian was somehow responsible for Snelling's death. To Dysart's way of thinking, it didn't make sense. But despite discreetly questioning everyone in the area he could think of, he'd been unable to prove otherwise—or to find anyone else who had a reason to do away with Snelling.

He returned to his desk, slumped in the chair, and propped his booted feet on the polished mahogany surface. Snelling had kept to himself at the inn. He was not seen speaking to anyone, aside from the servants, and the only questions the runner had asked had been inquiries about a young lady. Nor had he been seen meeting with a

127

suspicious stranger. As far as Dysart had been able to learn, there were not and had not been any strangers in the area, except for Andrew Marling.

Dysart was quite willing to consider Marling as a culprit, and had even sent his group up to Town to discover if the gentleman had any other reason for quitting London besides his pursuit of Miss Montague. But though Toby had unearthed a disgusting amount of gossip about Marling, the groom had found nothing that could possibly evoke the interest of Bow Street.

An impartial observer, Dysart thought, would be forced to conclude that the only person who benefited from Snelling's demise was Miss Spencer. The person who had the best opportunity to bash the runner over the head was Miss Spencer. But he was not impartial, and nothing would convince him that Juliana was responsible for Snelling's death.

A tap on the door caught his attention, and Lord Dysart glanced up expectantly. A second later he breathed a sigh of relief as he saw Charles Harrington step into the room. "Thank God you've come! What the devil took you so long?"

Charles, his shoulders aching from the strain of driving through the night, his drab green driving coat showing the dust and stains of travel, glanced at his employer and replied tiredly, "My apologies, my lord. I returned as quickly as possible."

Dysart came to his feet and circled around the desk, extending his hand in welcome. "Of course you did. I did not mean to imply otherwise. 'Tis just that I have been anxious for some word from you. But sit down—have you eaten? Shall I ring for something?"

"Thank you, but I want nothing," Charles said as he sprawled in one of the wing chairs. "With your permission, I shall seek my bed as soon as I tell you what I've

128

learned." He hesitated, then added, "I fear I have bad news."

Dysart filled two glasses from the crystal brandy decanter on his desk and carried one of them to his secretary. "Let me hear the worst."

Still mortified from his last experience with brandy, Charles waved the glass away. "I found Morcombe easily enough, but your friend Philip ... I am sorry, my lord, but he died over two years ago."

"I see," Dysart murmured, tightening the hold on his glass. He had suspected as much but hoped he was wrong. The confirmation now filled him with an aching regret. He had always meant to visit Philip, but there never seemed to be enough time and now ... now there wasn't any. Dysart swallowed some of the brandy, welcoming the burning warmth. After a moment, he faced Charles again. "What happened?"

"He was sailing on his yacht with his father. Apparently they were caught in a sudden storm. I spoke to one of the neighbors, who said there was no indication that it was anything but an unfortunate accident."

"And this Lucian that Miss Spencer mentioned. Did you find him?"

"Finding him was no problem," Charles answered with a weary sigh. "Getting anyone to speak about him, however, was what took so much time. The villagers at Morcombe are terrified of him, and the other landowners most reluctant to say a word against His Grace."

"His Grace?" Dysart echoed, his heavy brows arching upward.

Charles nodded. "A distant cousin, Lucian deVere inherited the title and the estates. The new Duke of Morcombe is a powerful man, my lord, and demands instant and total obedience from those around him. He is not well liked but he is feared. Indeed, it was only by swearing their confidence would be kept that I was able to persuade anyone to discuss the man. Even then, I had the feeling they were not telling me all they knew."

"That confirms what Miss Spencer said . . . was His Grace in residence?"

"I saw him several times, though only at a distance. He is driven through the village in an elegant gilded coach drawn by six powerful horses. I gather he enjoys displaying his wealth."

"A closed carriage driven by a groom does not necessarily signify the duke was within. He could have ordered his coachman to—"

"There can be no doubt, my lord," Charles interrupted. "As it happened, the duke's carriage nearly ran down a street urchin while I was in the village. His Grace was considerably upset and stuck his head out the window to rail at the unfortunate boy. The Duke of Morcombe is a young man, rather pale of complexion with piercing blue eyes. He makes it a habit to dress in black and cannot be mistaken."

"Is it possible that His Grace has just returned to Morcombe? Could he not have been in Chichester a fortnight ago?"

Charles shook his head. "Not according to the villagers. I found one lad willing to talk—for a sum. He will not testify to it, but he swears the Duke of Morcombe is behind much of the smuggling going on, and several ships have been seen putting into the cove late at night. One can see the flash of lights from the village—signals, my lad thinks. I saw them myself on two evenings. Rumor has it that His Grace is always present at such times and oversees the unloading himself. Two other villagers told me much the same. It appears His Grace has not left Morcombe in over a year."

"I see," Dysart murmured. He was disappointed but not surprised, for he had not believed it logical for Lucian to have done away with Snelling, though it made matters look all the blacker for Miss Spencer. He drained his glass, wondering briefly if it would not be better to dig up the runner and bury him somewhere in the depths of the woods where he would never be found. No one could convict Miss Spencer of his murder if there was no body . . . but he knew without ever proposing the scheme that she would never agree to it.

As it was, she was badly frightened someone would stumble across Snelling's body, and she'd twice suggested confessing all to the squire. Only Juliana's concern that Dysart would be implicated had kept her silent thus far, but he knew they could not conceal the runner's death much longer. Three days ago the innkeeper had sent word to Bow Street that Snelling had disappeared. A damnable coil, he thought, but there had to be an answer.

He glanced at Charles, his head resting against the back of the chair, his eyes fighting to stay open. "You have done well, and I shall not keep you much longer. Just tell me what you learned about Lady Juliana."

"I think your suspicions are correct, my lord. Lady Juliana was described much as one would Miss Spencer. According to the villagers, shortly after Lady Juliana's father and brother died, His Grace announced he would wed her . . . only she disappeared from Morcombe a week before the wedding. They say His Grace was furious. He posted a reward for information and when that failed, he set it about that she had fled with some priceless necklace—the Sunderland Diamonds, I believe he called it. Apparently, that was when he employed Bow Street to hunt her down."

"The cur! I should like to have a few words alone with His Grace."

"Careful, my lord," Charles warned. "The Duke of Morcombe is no gentleman. Several mysterious deaths along the coast are rumored to be his doing, though 'tis impossible to prove. His foes are set upon by thugs in the dead of night. Anyone gainsaying him suffers dreadful misfortunes—'tis why the villagers were so reluctant to speak of him."

"I shall bear it in mind," Dysart answered, but the grim look in his eyes boded ill for His Grace if ever their paths should cross. He remained at his desk long after Charles had retired, long after the candles had burned down, long after the brandy decanter was emptied. There had to be a way to absolve Miss Spencer of Snelling's death and to restore her rightful position.

At Blandings the week had passed pleasantly enough, if one discounted Damaris's initial railing at her confinement. She had treated the rest of the household to unseemly tantrums and behaved so rudely at dinner that her aunt threatened to have her meals served in the nursery. Damaris complained to Juliana, but her companion, preoccupied with her own concerns, only advised her to try for a little more conduct.

After one particularly unpleasant scene Monday evening, Damaris fled the house in tears and Mrs. Throckmorton retired to her room with a megrim. Oliver went after his cousin and found her in the garden, weeping uncontrollably. He offered his handkerchief, waited until her sobs had lessened, then asked, "How long do you mean to go on like this?"

"Until your mother comes to her senses," Damaris retorted, her green eyes flashing. "I cannot bear being locked up. 'Tis barbaric and I shall write to my uncle and tell him how shabbily I am treated."

Oliver laughed. "Do. I hope he will be sympathetic, though I seem to recall that when Mama wrote to him that you were here, he replied that he wished never to set eyes on you again."

She flushed. "Only because I ran away, and even Aunt Caroline did not blame me for that because Uncle Edward was trying to force me to marry my cousin. And I do not scruple to tell you he was a pig. I would never marry him."

"I see. And is that how you intend to describe me to your uncle?"

She laughed. "Pray do not be absurd. You are a great deal nicer than Henry. Besides, you have no wish to marry me."

"None at all," he agreed.

"Well you need not sound so smug about it. There are dozens of gentlemen who would adore to marry me."

Oliver lounged against the railing and watched his cousin seated on the stone bench in the center of the garden. Even after crying as she had, Damaris still looked incredibly lovely. Her long blond hair was worn loose today and tumbled about her shoulders in disarray that should have looked messy but instead gave her a look of enchanting innocence. Her long lashes were darkened by the wet tears, and anguish lent a tinge of color to her high cheekbones. To anyone who did not know her, she looked like an angel—an impression Oliver knew had no basis in reality, but that nevertheless caused him to speak more kindly than was his wont. "I know you are not without suitors, Cousin. I only hope that when you choose one, it will be a gentleman who truly cares for you and not just for your fortune."

Mistaking his concern for criticism, she glared at him and replied furiously, "If you are referring to Andrew, he *does* care for me."

"I doubt it," Oliver said gently. "If he did, he would not ask you to meet him clandestinely."

"I am sure I do not know what you are talking about. Andrew is—"

"Cut line," Oliver interrupted. "I know a great deal more than you think, including the times you have stolen out of the house late at night to meet him. But you needn't worry. I don't intend to rat on you. 'Tis no concern of mine if you wish to ruin yourself."

Damaris would not meet his eyes. She turned away and shrugged her shoulders. "If Aunt Caroline were not so Gothic, I would not be forced to meet Andrew on the sly. But she refuses to allow him to call."

"My mother, despite what you may think, cares about you. She knows Marling for a gazetted fortune hunter. Lord, Damaris, I never thought you lacking in wit, but if you can't see what's in front of your eyes, well, the pair of you deserve each other."

"Thank you very much, Oliver," she retorted, rising. She lifted her head proudly but her luminous eyes shimmered with tears and her small, round chin trembled.

"Egad, don't start the waterworks again. I only came out here to tell you that if you want to get around Mama, you are going about it in the wrong way."

"Why should you care?" she demanded suspiciously.

"In truth I don't, but I am growing tired of having the house in a constant uproar. Look, Damaris, all you have to do is behave a bit more like Melody. Be civil and tell Mama you're sorry. She dislikes confining you to the house, but your conduct makes it impossible for her to relent. Behave for a day or so, then apologize to Mama and the entire episode will be forgotten."

"Do you really think so?"

"Trust me," he said, grinning down at her. "I've learned from experience, and I shall give you one more bit of advice. Pay some attention to Charles Harrington. I cannot fathom why, but he is smitten with you."

Her eyes widened as she stared at Oliver in surprise. She had not seen Harrington in nearly a week, and she'd thought it was because he'd taken exception to her remarks about Pamela. Aloud she said, "Surely, you jest. Mr. Harrington is nearly as stuffy as Aunt Caroline, and he . . . he seems to disapprove of me."

"You have it wrong, Cousin. He does not like some of the things you do—but all the same he will not hear a word said against you. I have the feeling that if Harrington were to ask to take you for a drive, Mama would not refuse permission."

On Tuesday, Damaris took her cousin's advice to heart and conducted herself so angelically that her aunt stared at her in nervous anticipation of a new outburst. But her niece continued to behave so sweetly, so much like a well-bred young lady, that Mrs. Throckmorton finally remarked to Miss Spencer, "There, you must own that I was right, my dear. All Damaris needed was a firm hand."

Juliana eyed her charge warily, knowing it was unlikely the girl had reformed overnight. She found Damaris's sudden transformation cause more for alarm than relief, but she could not deny the change was a welcome one. Of course it helped that Melody and Oliver had ridden out with a party from the vicarage, so there was no one present to provoke Damaris into unseemly behavior.

The morning passed most agreeably and when Lord Dysart and Charles Harrington called late that afternoon, Damaris continued to conduct herself in an exemplary manner and treated Mr. Harrington with such a flattering degree of attention that Mrs. Throckmorton congratulated herself on her strategy. Feeling absurdly pleased with both herself and her niece, she suggested the young people take Faustus and enjoy a stroll in the gardens.

The sheepdog, who had been lying across one of Dysart's boots, immediately bounded to his feet and nudged his lordship's knee. Juliana decided Faustus did not need a leash since they would not go beyond the boundary of the gardens, and she knew it was most unlikely that the dog would stray far from Lord Dysart's side.

For once, Damaris did not protest taking Faustus along, and as they were about to leave the room, she even turned back to say sweetly to her aunt, "Are you certain you will not come with us? Or, if you like, I could stay and bear you company."

Mrs. Throckmorton beamed at her. "Thank you, my dear. 'Tis most thoughtful of you to ask, but I shall just sit here and close my eyes for a few moments. You run along."

Damaris and Charles Harrington led the way across the terrace, and as Dysart followed more slowly with Juliana, he bent his head to whisper teasingly, "Confess, Miss Spencer, what have you done with the real Miss Montague?"

She smiled dutifully but did not answer.

Dysart observed her silently for a moment. She was clad, as was her custom, in a simple white muslin day dress, adorned only by a deep green ribbon beneath the bodice. Across her shoulders she'd draped a fine cashmere shawl, but it was slightly faded and worn in spots. Her deep auburn hair, glinting in the sun with coppery lights, might have offset such a dowdy ensemble but she'd bound it up in a prim knot at the nape of her neck. At first glance, she seemed the plain governess she wished the world to think her, but nothing could really disguise her true beauty or the air of regality she unconsciously assumed.

It was only when she turned her head to look up at Dysart that he noticed the shadows beneath her turquoise eyes and the tense look about her mouth. Slowing his pace, he allowed Charles to draw Miss Montague slightly ahead, then asked softly, "What is troubling you, my dear?"

Juliana's composure suddenly snapped. She had not

slept well for the past week. The constant worry that one of the gardeners might discover Snelling, and her conviction that Lucian lurked nearby waiting to do her harm, had preyed on her nerves until she was at her wits' end. In light of her predicament, Lord Dysart's question seemed ludicrous.

Her voice low and rife with sarcasm, she retorted, "Why nothing, my lord, save that there is a strange man buried less than ten feet away, a man whose death will undoubtedly be laid at my door. Of course, 'tis a lovely day and undoubtedly I am foolish to allow such concerns to weigh with me. I must beg your pardon if I seemed unduly distracted."

"It is I who should apologize," he murmured, watching the way anger turned her eyes a deeper blue. "I did not mean to make light of your worries. Indeed, I have thought of little else."

Annoyed with herself for railing at his lordship when he had tried only to help, Juliana sighed. "Forgive me, my lord, and pray forget what I said. You have been more than kind. I do not deserve your help."

"You deserve a great deal more, but we shall discuss that another time. At the moment, we have more pressing concerns." Her hand rested on the crook of his arm, and with gentle persuasion he led her to a bench. "Sit down, my dear. I hesitate to add to your burdens, but I believe you must know what has occurred so that you will be prepared."

Her heart sinking, Juliana glanced up at him. She knew Dysart had been questioning people in the neighborhood, knew he had been seeking someone with a motive to murder Snelling. Her gravest fear was that he had found her cousin, a man who frightened her beyond belief. Trying to keep her voice calm, she asked, "Is it Lucian? Is he here?"

"No . . . as far as I have been able to discover, no one

has seen a stranger in the neighborhood. We cannot find anyone with the slightest reason to wish Snelling ill. In truth, Miss Spencer, I almost wish someone *had* seen your mysterious Lucian, but he is not—and has not been—here. From what I have been able to discover, your cousin has not left his home in over a year."

It took a moment for the meaning of his words to penetrate her consciousness, then she looked up at him curiously. "How can you know that, Lord Dysart? I do not recall telling you where my cousin lived."

"It seems there are a great many things you neglected to tell me . . . Lady Juliana."

She paled slightly, but her gaze remained fixed unflinchingly on his. "That, sir, is a title I do not choose to claim."

"Why did you not tell me the truth?" he asked. His voice held no anger, only an aching sadness that added a poignancy to his words. "Did you think I would betray you? Surely, as Philip's sister, you must know that we were once close friends, good friends. If you had notified me of his death, I would have come to your assistance."

She glanced down at her hands, clasped tightly in her lap. "I did write to you when Philip died . . . I wrote to a number of his friends. My cousin said he would frank my letters, and it . . . it was several months before I learned he had burned them instead."

Faustus, reacting to the pain and despair in her voice, whimpered and licked at her fingers.

Juliana unconsciously caressed the dog's silky ears, then glanced up at Dysart. "My brother spoke of you often, my lord. He admired you greatly and said one could not have a better friend. I knew that if I confided in you, you would not betray me, but I kept silent because I saw no use in raking up the past. You can do nothing for Philip now."

"Except watch over his little sister," Dysart answered

as he sat down beside her. He nudged Faustus aside and took her hands in his. "Philip would expect it of me, so let me hear no arguments on that score. When this business is done, I shall take you to my mother. You will enjoy an extended visit with her, and then, between us all, we shall decide what is best for you in the future."

She opened her mouth to protest, but he stopped her words with a gentle finger on her lips. "I will not take no for an answer. Are we agreed?"

"You leave me little choice."

"Good. 'Tis time you realized that," he teased. "Now, the first thing we must do is find a way to clear your name. I thought that—"

"I have told you, my lord, I cannot confront Lucian. Do not ask it of me."

"You can and you must, and I shall help you. Do not fret, my dear. Lucian may be a powerful man, but I am not without influence or means. I have already thought of a way your cousin might be induced to drop the charges against you. It will require a visit to Morcombe, but—"

"Please do not go there, my lord," she pleaded. "I have lost my father, my brother, and my friends. I could not bear it if Lucian harmed you, and he is . . . he is vindictive."

"Allow me to worry about your cousin. I told you, I have a plan, but I want your promise that you will do nothing foolish while I am gone." He paused, drew a deep breath, then told her, "The innkeeper has informed Bow Street of Snelling's disappearance. Although he was working on his own, I suspect they will send another runner to investigate."

Juliana closed her eyes for a brief moment. "What . . . what shall we do? If they find the body—"

"Do not start fretting about that," Dysart advised. "I am nearly certain it will be some time before another runner arrives, and by then we may know more. I do not want to raise your hopes unduly, but I believe I know what happened to Snelling."

"Tell me," she implored.

"As soon as I know for certain. I must—" He broke off, staring beyond her, and then muttered a curse before raising his voice and calling, "Faustus! Come here, fellow. Come on, boy."

Juliana turned and gasped as she saw the large sheepdog busily sniffing the area around the sundial. His tail wagging furiously, the dog started to dig in the garden. He looked in their direction when Dysart called to him, but after a few seconds resumed his digging.

"Good heavens, what is all the commotion?" Damaris asked, coming around the curve of the path with Charles Harrington.

"Faustus is . . . digging up the garden," Juliana replied, her voice faint. "Your aunt will not appreciate it if he disturbs the roses."

"I will fetch him," Dysart said and strode determinedly toward the sheepdog.

"Oh, pooh. He is probably after an old bone he buried. That dog is always digging up something," Damaris said, turning to Charles with a dazzling smile. "You would not credit some of the things he brings into the house. Why, a few months ago, we were all sitting in the drawing room and Faustus dragged in a dead squirrel and deposited it right at Melody's feet. Can you imagine? I was positively ill."

Charles looked more than a little ill himself. "Perhaps I should help his lordship." But Dysart had found a stick and tossed it away from the sundial, with orders for the dog to fetch. Faustus bounded after it, then carried it proudly to his lordship as he rejoined the others on the terrace.

"Such a fuss over that silly dog," Damaris murmured, then turned to Juliana with a pleading look. "Miss

Spencer, do you think my aunt will allow Mr. Harrington to take me driving tomorrow?"

"I doubt she will have any objection," Juliana replied. Glad of an excuse to get the dog safely back inside, she suggested, "Let us ask her."

Nodding happily, Damaris led the way. Engrossed in her conversation with Charles, she didn't notice that Dysart lagged behind, or the way he whispered urgently to Miss Spencer.

"Try to keep that blasted dog out of the gardens."

"I thought you were fond of Faustus," Juliana murmured.

Dysart didn't bother responding to that but warned her, "I shall leave for Morcombe this evening. With luck, I will return by Friday. If you run into problems, trust Charles to help you."

"Miss Spencer, are you coming?" Damaris called imperiously.

"Yes, dear," Juliana replied while trying to free her hand from Dysart's grasp.

"I shall be glad when you are no longer at that child's beck and call," he muttered. "Juliana, promise me you will do nothing foolish until I return."

"My lord, I must go in—"

"Your promise," he demanded.

"If anyone is imperious," she began but relented when she gazed into his dark eyes. Eyes that reflected all his concern and care for her. "Very well, my lord, you have my promise, but I suggest you return as quickly as possible."

Chapter 10

The days passed with agonizing slowness for Juliana.
It seemed the fates had conspired to leave her with too
much time to dwell on her situation. Melody visited the
vicarage at every opportunity, which may have been due
to the presence of Mr. Evans, the new curate, with whom
she seemed taken. And Oliver had begun calling on
Charlotte Chadleigh, an occurrence his mother viewed
with mixed feelings. Miss Chadleigh was a very nice
young lady, well mannered, deferential to her elders,
obedient . . . she would make a charming daughter-
in-law. But, unfortunately, she had a very small dowry,
particularly so when compared to that of Oliver's cousin.

"Of course I wish him to be happy," Mrs. Throckmorton lamented to Juliana on Thursday afternoon when
Oliver sent a message home that he would dine, again, at
the Chadleighs'. "But I do not see why he could not be
sensible enough to develop an attachment for Damaris."

"I believe the relationship is too close," Juliana replied
with a smile. "You have said yourself that they are more
like brother and sister than cousins. Only think how they
would argue if they were to wed."

"True, my dear, but she has been so agreeable since
our little talk. Why, they have hardly quarreled at all the
past few days."

"Oliver has not been at home sufficiently long to give
her opportunity," Juliana replied dryly.

The widow sighed. "I had hopes they would reach an understanding, but I suppose they are not at all suited. Still, such a pity to see a fortune go out of the family—not that Oliver is in need of it. No, indeed. Mr. Throckmorton left him comfortably fixed, and from what his man of business told me, the income from his investments should only increase . . . but it would have been lovely. I only pray she does not waste it on some scoundrel like Marling. I do not think I could bear it. Every sensibility must be offended."

"I think you no longer need be concerned about him, Mrs. Throckmorton," Juliana replied as she finished setting a neat row of tiny stitches. "He was at Miss Milhouse's when we called, and unless I am much mistaken, Damaris took pains to avoid him."

"Oh, my dear, I do hope you are right. My gravest fear has been that she might elope with him. You know how . . . impulsive she is, and she was so very angry when I confined her to the house. Thank goodness that is all behind us now. Tell me, do you think her sincerely attached to Mr. Harrington? This is the third day she has driven out with him."

"She has not confided in me," Juliana hedged. She herself was unable to decide if Damaris was merely using Charles Harrington as a means of escaping the house or if she sincerely liked the young man. She hoped it was the latter.

"Well, he may be a younger son and I know her uncle will think it a dreadful misalliance, but all the same I pray something comes of it. Damaris seems willing to heed his advice when she will not listen to anyone else, and that, my dear, I don't scruple to tell you, that alone would make him entirely acceptable in my eyes."

"Mr. Harrington is not entirely without expectations, ma'am. Lord Dysart told me he expects to see him in the House of Commons one day, and there is no telling how

143

far he may rise. I believe his lordship intends to sponsor him."

"Hmmph. I do not mean to say anything against Lord Dysart, for all the world knows he has been utterly charming to me. However, considering his lordship's reputation, I cannot help but think that Mr. Harrington would do well to find another sponsor. Although I must say I find it increasingly difficult to believe the gossip one hears about his lordship. Certainly his behavior has been unexceptional since he came to Chichester. . . . Perhaps he has found a reason to reform his ways."

Juliana felt the blood rushing to her cheeks, and her neat row of stitches suddenly took an erratic turn.

"Oh dear, now I have embarrassed you. Mr. Throckmorton always said I had about as much delicacy as a blacksmith. I hope you will forgive me."

"There is nothing to forgive, ma'am, but I fear your imagination has persuaded you to place too much significance on what has been mere kindness and civility from his lordship."

The widow shook her head. "If you truly believe that, Miss Spencer, you are not as up to snuff as I thought. Trust me. One does not reach my years without learning a thing or two, and 'tis plain to me that his lordship has a marked preference for you—and if you were to ask my opinion, I would say he would be most fortunate were you to have him."

"Now *that* would be a misalliance," Juliana replied in an attempt to make light of the situation.

"Balderdash! I have never inquired about your family or asked how you came to be in need of employment, but I know enough to be certain you come of good stock and were raised like a lady, and I will tell you something else, Miss Spencer. Mr. Harrington told me himself, the first night he and Lord Dysart dined here, that he expected to be at Windward for only a week or so, but his lordship is still here, and I can think of only one reason he would dally in a village like Chichester."

Juliana could think of nothing to say, and when Melody's sheepdog chose that moment to lumber to his feet and look pitifully at the windows, she seized on the dog as an excuse. "Will you excuse me, ma'am? It appears as though Faustus needs an outing."

"If you wish, my dear, but you could just turn him out. I don't see why you should add to your duties by walking him—the way that animal eats, 'tis certain he won't stray far from the house."

"I do not mind, truly, and the gardeners have been complaining about Faustus digging in the flower beds." This was not strictly true, but Juliana salved her conscience with the knowledge that they would have complained had they seen the sheepdog digging furiously in the roses. She snapped his leash on him and led him outside, walking determinedly away from the sundial.

With the sun setting, the day was a trifle chilly to be out without a shawl, but Juliana welcomed the rush of cool air on her flushed cheeks. Mrs. Throckmorton was an incurable matchmaker, but she was not precisely impartial. Juliana, who had thought of little else for the past few days, knew that it was only her employer's partiality that made her imagine Lord Dysart intended anything more than kindness. Her employer might see nothing incongruous in an earl offering for a governess without dowry or name, but Juliana knew how inappropriate such a match would be. She knew, too, that Dysart, in the way that gentlemen tended to do, believed himself somehow responsible for his friend's little sister. He meant to see her through this mess she'd got herself into, but it was not because he thought of her in a romantic way.

He had never even attempted to kiss her, and a man of his reputation would surely have tried if he was the least attracted to her. Thoughts of what it would be like if he *had* kissed her brought a deeper blush to her cheeks. She had not received many kisses in her twenty-three years, other than the gentle pecks on her cheek from father and brother. A few gentlemen had tried, but those had been clumsy attempts, the men clutching at her as though she were a fish on a line. Dysart would be more skillful. What had Damaris said when they'd first met him? His smile had seduced more ladies . . . Devil Dysart, she'd called him.

He would be gentle yet masterful, he would be—

"Faustus, no!" Juliana commanded, pulling sharply on his lead as the sheepdog lunged after a squirrel that had darted across the path. The dog nearly escaped her, which she thought would have served her right after daydreaming about something she had no business even thinking of. Poor Faustus looked crestfallen when she made him heel beside her. Guiltily, Juliana knelt and caressed his ears. "I know you despise being leashed, but if you are a good fellow, then perhaps tomorrow I will take you to the woods and let you run a bit."

Damaris sat contentedly in the gig, watching Charles Harrington as he effortlessly handled his team. Like everything else he did, he drove the horses competently—no showiness, no riding to an inch in passing other carriages, no racing. He treated Damaris as though she were some special cargo he was privileged to carry. For her, the past three days had been a new experience. Gentlemen had always flocked to court her, of course, but though they flattered, teased, and tried to seduce her, none had ever . . . cherished her. It was the only word she could think of to describe the way Charles made her feel. Cherished. She liked the notion and smiled to herself.

Charles glanced at her to make certain she was settled

comfortably and the sun was not in her eyes. Seeing her smile, he asked, "What amuses you, Damaris?"

"I was just thinking how surprised my uncle would be if he could see me now," she replied.

"I suppose he would think me an unsuitable escort. I am aware that—"

Her sudden laughter rang out, startling him. "Dear Charles, you have it the wrong way around. Uncle Edward would be astonished that so proper a gentleman, so respectable a person as yourself, would have aught to do with me. He thinks I am . . . incorrigible."

"Then he does not know you," Charles replied in the confident way he had, as though that quite settled the matter.

It was utterances such as that that had endeared him to Damaris, which made her want to be as good as Charles believed her. She smiled at him, a smile of such angelic beauty and sweetness, he caught his breath and for a few seconds forgot he was driving a high-strung pair of thoroughbreds.

"Charles! You must not look at me like that."

"I cannot help it, my dear, not when you—drat, there should be a law against carriages traveling at such a reckless pace," he muttered as a high-perch phaeton barreled down upon them. It was clear the other driver meant to pass, and Charles maneuvered his horses as far to the right as he could.

The phaeton thundered past, kicking up a cloud of dust, and Charles cursed silently. It was a moment before he realized the other driver had slowed and pulled his carriage across the road. "It is Marling," he informed Damaris. "And it appears he wants a word with you. Do you wish to speak with him?"

The question was asked courteously, without the least hint of censure, but she knew Charles disapproved of her association with Marling, and it was Charles she wanted to please. Suddenly shy, she shook her head. Andrew was part of another world, part of a lot of things Damaris wished only to forget.

As they neared the high-perch phaeton, Marling looked down at them and called out, "Damaris, I must have a word with you." Glaring at Charles, he added, "In private, if you please."

"The lady does not wish to speak with you," Charles replied. "Be good enough to move your carriage so that we may pass."

Marling stared at Damaris, who refused to meet his eyes, then at Harrington, who had blocked every attempt he'd made to speak to the chit alone in the last few days. Anger surged in him as he thought of the amount of time and funds he'd invested in wooing the heiress. He could ill afford to have her draw back now.

Nor could he believe that he'd been cut out by this stodgy, bookish secretary. Had it been Lord Dysart, with his good looks and unconscious charm, Marling could understand it. But Harrington had neither style nor elegance. He lacked town bronze and was, in short, as dull as a dog. Damaris could not possibly prefer him to his own sophisticated, fashionable self. She must, he thought, be trying to pay him back for spending so much time with Cressy Milhouse.

Convinced he'd found the answer to this puzzle, Andrew laughed and called to Damaris, "My sweet, I know you are angry with me, but can we not discuss it in private? Tell your . . . your driver to set you down." Confident of her reply, he tossed the reins to his groom and climbed down.

As he strode toward them, Damaris whispered to Charles, "Can we not drive around his carriage?"

"Too risky," Charles replied softly. "I would do nothing to endanger you, but you need have no fear he will bother you. Hold the reins, please."

"Wh-what are you going to do?"

"Teach him some much-needed manners."

She started to protest but he hushed her and climbed down, turning to face the interloper. Charles had to look up at him, for Marling was taller by a head, but he showed no fear as he repeated calmly, "The lady does not wish to converse with you. I am asking you again to please move your carriage."

"And what are you going to do about it if I don't?"

Charles sighed and took a half step backward.

"Having second thoughts?" Marling taunted, but he'd barely gotten the words out of his mouth before a well-aimed and powerful fist landed beneath his chin. The force of the blow sent him sprawling, and he very much feared a tooth had been knocked loose. Still slightly dazed, he rubbed his jaw and stared up at Harrington.

"I boxed at Oxford," Charles said almost apologetically.

"A lucky punch—you caught me off guard!"

"Should you care to try again?"

Marling glared at him. He was not in the habit of fighting, and Harrington had obviously had a great deal of experience. As he came to his feet, he glanced up at Damaris, then muttered, "I do not brawl in front of ladies. If you wish to settle this like gentlemen, I shall meet you."

"Wonderful. Name the time and place, though perhaps I should mention that I studied fencing as well and am accounted an excellent shot."

"You don't scare me, Harrington."

"I never intended to. All I want is for you to remove your carriage from the road."

"I will—as soon as I speak to Damaris."

"I have told you, sir, the lady does not wish to speak to you. Now either move your carriage, or I shall be forced to move it for you."

Marling backed up a step or two. He was being made

149

to look a fool, and fury goaded him. Losing his temper, he shouted, "She's no lady. Ask her about the times we have met secretly. She was planning to elope with me before you—" Marling's words were cut short as Harrington grasped his stock and twisted it until he could no longer breathe. Marling clutched at the hands surrounding his throat, but they were as inflexible as iron. He felt himself being moved inexorably backward.

"I never wish to hear Miss Montague's name on your lips again. Is that quite clear, Mr. Marling?"

"I . . . I can't breathe!"

"Is it clear?"

Helplessly, Marling nodded. His eyes were watering and his throat felt rubbed raw. He would have agreed to anything to get Harrington's hands off his neck.

"Thank you. Now I suggest you get in your carriage and continue on your way before I forget there is a lady present."

Released abruptly, Marling staggered toward his carriage. His groom leaned down to give him a hand up, but he ignored it. When he was finally safely aboard, with one hand still soothing his throat, he muttered hoarsely, "Drive on, you fool."

Charles stood in the center of the road, watching until the high-perch phaeton drew away. He straightened the ruffle of lace at his cuffs, adjusted his collar, then returned to his own carriage. "I apologize, my dear. You should never have been made to witness such a barbaric display."

She gazed at him with awe. "I . . . I never imagined you could . . . could fight like that."

"I am not proud of it," he replied, though a small part of him was extremely pleased that he had acquitted himself so well in front of her. "My father believed a gentleman skillful in speech was much stronger than a man adept with his fists—but he made certain my brothers and

I were capable of defending ourselves ... and our ladies."

A warm glow filled Damaris and she sat silently for a moment. He had done it again—made her feel as though she were someone special, made her feel cherished. But then she recollected Marling's parting words. She worried her bottom lip with her teeth as she considered what to say. "Charles, I ... I feel I owe you an explanation. I did meet Andrew Marling secretly, and more than once."

"If you did so, I am certain you had sufficient reason, but you need not explain."

She smiled. "Thank you, but I should like you to know the truth. You see, when I first came here from London, Aunt Caroline let it be known that I had run away from my uncle's home. Everyone looked at me as though they were ... were just waiting for me to do something outrageous. Even Mrs. Trilby, the vicar's wife, pitied me. I knew that even if I tried, I could never be as good as her Pamela or my cousin Melody. And then Andrew followed me here. He approved of what I had done, and he encouraged me. He made fun of my aunt and Oliver and said the people here were all yokels and could not appreciate anyone who had lived in London. I wanted to believe him. I know it was foolish, but he made me feel good, and when my aunt refused to allow him to call, I agreed to meet him."

"I see. And now?"

"Now I realize that Andrew cared nothing for me. He only wanted control of my fortune. He kept trying to persuade me to elope."

"But you did not, that is the important thing," Charles assured her. "And for that I am most thankful."

She sighed blissfully. "So am I."

Damaris invited Charles to come in when they arrived at Blandings late that afternoon, and while he was speaking to Miss Spencer, she quietly asked her aunt to invite him to dinner.

Mrs. Throckmorton agreed at once and Mr. Harrington accepted, saying that he hoped it would not be too much trouble. She dismissed such a notion as absurd and sent a maid to the kitchen to inform her chef that another place was to be laid. In truth, Mrs. Throckmorton never hesitated to increase her numbers for dinner, for she employed an excellent cook and left the planning of meals entirely to his discretion. That he might not wish to have his arrangements altered at the last moment never occurred to her, and she would have been most astonished to know of his annoyance.

Considering the matter settled, she inquired of Mr. Harrington, "May we expect Lord Dysart to return soon? I vow we have grown so accustomed to having him in our midst that his presence is sorely missed."

"We have hopes that he will return on the morrow, ma'am," he replied and, after a sympathetic glance at Miss Spencer, added, "I have little doubt that he would much prefer to be here."

"Well, Chichester may not be a metropolis like London, but we do contrive to amuse ourselves tolerably well—ah, here is my daughter, and Mr. Evans. My dear, I rather thought you meant to remain at the vicarage for dinner."

Melody, accompanied by the vicar's new curate, turned a deep shade of pink. Juliana came to her rescue and introduced Mr. Evans to Charles Harrington. The two men sized each other up and, both being of like natures, were soon deep in conversation.

Geoffrey Evans was tall and extremely thin. His dark brown hair refused to lie in ordered neatness but fell over his wide brow so that he was constantly brushing it back in place. Thin brows arched over light brown eyes and a long nose that gave the young curate a studious look.

Mrs. Throckmorton thought he looked undernourished and said as much to Miss Spencer. "Though one cannot be surprised, for however much I may admire Mrs. Trilby, I would starve within a fortnight were I forced to dine at the vicarage every evening. Melody, my lamb, do ask Mr. Evans if he would care to stay for dinner."

The gentleman, when appealed to, hesitated. "I should not like to impose, ma'am, or upset your table."

"I assure you 'tis not the least problem," his hostess answered with sanguine confidence and rang the bell. When Emily appeared, she was once again dispatched to the kitchen to inform the chef to lay two more places for dinner.

She reappeared in the drawing room a few moments later and spoke softly to Miss Spencer, who excused herself and followed the maid into the hall.

"I'm sorry, Miss Spencer, but Cook said 'tis impossible to stretch a meal for three to accommodate six."

"Make it seven," Juliana said with a sigh as Oliver entered the long hall. "Never mind, I shall have a word with Jean-Claude myself." She waved to Oliver but did not stop to speak with him, hurrying instead down the long hall and belowstairs to the kitchen. She could hear the chef as she drew near, his voice rising in impassioned French as it did whenever he was upset.

"*Mon Dieu!* I should never have come to this primitive land. I am among the philistines!" He turned to Juliana as soon as she entered the room and let loose a torrent of French with such rapidity, she had difficulty following his words. But she understood sufficient to know none of it was flattering.

"In English, if you please," she told him calmly.

"Madam asks the impossible," he complained, waving a cleaver in the air for emphasis. "I plan dinner for *trois*—three, you comprehend, three of the little hens, three of the fishes, but now she asks for six!"

153

"Not six," she began.

"Ah, mademoiselle, you relieve me. A miracle I would have—"

"Seven," Juliana said, raising her voice slightly to be heard above his. And after she'd stunned him into silence, she said, "I am sorry, Monsieur Claude, but I am confident that one as talented as yourself, as creative as only a Frenchman can be, will find a way to contrive."

He threw his hands into the air. "Who could contrive such a thing? The hens, they are nearly done—"

"Very well. I shall tell Mrs. Throckmorton you cannot oblige her."

The rotund Frenchman thought rapidly. He was extremely well paid, and there were few houses where the chef had entire control over the kitchen. Mrs. Throckmorton might be a philistine, but she never interfered. As Juliana reached the door, he called, "Wait! I should not like to disappoint Madam, but I shall need time, mademoiselle. Tell her dinner must be set back an hour."

"Half an hour," Juliana bargained. She added persuasively, "In an hour, the guests will be starving, their appetites all the keener."

"Half an hour," he agreed morosely.

She hurried from the kitchen before the chef could think of further arguments and prayed no one else would decide to visit. She encountered Oliver on the stairs as she went up to the drawing room.

"Is our cook rebelling? I could hear him from the hall."

"No more than usual," she replied tiredly. "I suppose he is not accustomed to households where the dinners are arranged so haphazardly."

"And I have added to your problems by coming home after telling Mama I would be dining with the Chadleighs. I would not have done so, but I heard something rather strange that I thought you should know about."

"More gossip?" she asked, pausing in the hall.

"No, but it's likely to stir up some. A Bow Street Runner called at the Chadleighs' while I was there. He asked a lot of questions about a young lady, and from his description—well, she sounded amazingly like you."

Chapter 11

Juliana glanced up expectantly when the drawing-room door opened, but it was only Oliver. He greeted her carelessly, dropped a kiss on his mother's brow, then stretched out in a chair near the windows. "You should have ridden with us this morning, Miss Spencer. We had a capital time."

"Who did you ride with, dear?" Mrs. Throckmorton asked.

Spared the effort of a reply, Juliana studied Oliver. His casual words the night before had shattered her peace. She had been unable to sleep, and every time she heard a carriage, or the door open, she braced herself for a confrontation with a Bow Street Runner. Oliver, however, appeared blissfully unaware of the catastrophe about to befall the house. He had eaten an enormous breakfast, then ridden out with Melody and Damaris. Apparently, somewhere along the way, the trio had encountered Mr. Evans and Charles Harrington.

Her attention arrested, Juliana listened carefully, hoping for some mention of Lord Dysart. She had prayed last night his lordship would return this morning. Not that he could *do* anything, but any inquisition from a Bow Street Runner would not be nearly as frightening if Dysart were present.

Oliver, however, was talking about how splendidly the new chestnut he'd bought had performed. "And, Mama, you will not credit it, but Mel took several jumps, just as though she'd been doing it all her life."

"Did she?" his mother asked, unimpressed. She knew her daughter preferred not to jump, but as she herself did not ride, she saw nothing remarkable in that, and only inquired where his sister was now.

"She and Damaris are abovestairs changing. Mr. Evans promised to call this afternoon, and Charles will be here as well, unless his lordship has need of him."

Juliana held her breath.

"Has his lordship returned, then?" Mrs. Throckmorton asked obligingly.

Oliver nodded. "Early this morning. Oh, Miss Spencer, I nearly forgot. Charles said to tell you that Lord Dysart sends his regards, and he hopes to have the pleasure of seeing you later today."

Both relieved and embarrassed, Juliana bowed her head and murmured a thank-you. It seemed impossible that Dysart had been absent only four days. The time had passed unbearably slowly. Without realizing it, she had come to rely on him, come to expect his cheerful and irreverent presence, taking it as much for granted as she did the sun rising. It was extremely foolish of her to depend on him so greatly, foolish to have let him invade her heart so completely. She knew it, and yet she felt so much better just knowing he had returned. Now, if only Dysart would arrive at Blandings before the runner.

The door to the drawing room opened and she started, but it was only Damaris and Melody—for once talking companionably. Mrs. Throckmorton rang for fresh tea, then listened with patience to her daughter's description of her morning ride.

Melody, now attired in a charming sprigged muslin day dress, looked as fresh and sweet as a bouquet of summer flowers. Her brown eyes sparkled and her excitement lent a becoming touch of pink to her cheeks. "It was wonderful, Mama. Mr. Evans rode with me and I had not the least fear of falling. I never thought taking a jump could be so easy."

"Even though Oliver and I have been telling you that for the last year," Damaris teased. "But I suppose our assurances do not carry the same conviction as that of a certain curate who has the Lord on his side."

"Damaris Anne Montague! I will not have you taking our Lord's name so lightly."

Both girls giggled, and Damaris apologized. "I did not mean any disrespect, Aunt Caroline, but if you had seen my little cousin batting her lashes at Mr. Evans—"

"Damaris, I never did," Melody protested. Aware of her mother's curious eyes, she hastily made a show of coaxing Faustus from behind Juliana's chair and fussed over the sheepdog.

The knocker sounded. Juliana, her eyes riveted to the door and every muscle in her body strained to the point of tautness, did not notice Melody stroll toward the tall windows leading to the terrace—or that she opened one and allowed Faustus to bound outside.

Wilfred tapped on the drawing-room door, and a few seconds later opened it to announce Mr. Evans's arrival. Confusion reigned as Emily entered on his heels with the tea tray, followed only moments later by Charles Harrington's arrival. When a semblance of order was restored, Juliana accepted a fresh cup of tea from Mrs. Throckmorton and broke off a small piece of a wafer to feed to Faustus. Realizing the dog was no longer in the room, she noticed the window standing open. Alarmed, she questioned Melody.

"Oh, I let him out for a run. 'Tis such a beautiful day, I know he would much prefer to be outside. But you need not worry, Miss Spencer. Faustus will not wander off."

Juliana set aside her tea and rose from her chair. "I am far more concerned that he will destroy the rose garden. I shall fetch him and put him on his lead."

"Pray do not bother, Miss Spencer," Mrs. Throckmorton ordered. "After all, I pay the gardeners extremely well, and they have not sufficient to do just at present, while you are kept much too busy. Indeed, Mrs. Trilby was saying only yesterday that you looked rather tired. I suspect she feels I am taking advantage of you."

"No one who knows you could possibly think so, ma'am," Juliana replied, reluctantly resuming her seat. She could not go after the dog now—not without creating a fuss. She prayed Faustus would find a squirrel or rabbit to chase, and stay out of the garden.

Charles, who correctly read her concern, sat down beside her and encouraged her in a low voice, "Hold tight, Miss Spencer. His lordship will be here soon. I did not see him when he arrived, but he left word for me that he had good news."

Taking comfort from his words, she settled in her chair and drank a little of the tea. The hot and soothing warmth of the sweet liquid helped calm her nerves somewhat, and she was able to answer Charles's questions with tolerable composure. She knew he stayed beside her, talking idly of London and the coming Season, merely to set her at ease. Although she felt grateful for the diversion, she could not help noticing the way his gaze kept straying across the room to where Damaris was seated primly beside her cousin.

Sweet of him to stay, Juliana thought. She was about to suggest he go talk to the girls, when Wilfred stepped into the room. The butler glanced fleetingly in her direction, then crossed to speak in a low voice to Mrs. Throckmorton.

"I beg your pardon, Madam, but a *person* from the

159

Bow Street Magistrate's Court is here and insisting on a word with you."

"Bow Street?" she echoed in astonishment. Everyone in the room turned to look at her, and she hastily moderated her voice. "Well, whatever his business is, tell him he shall have to call later."

"I told him you were entertaining guests, Madam," Wilfred replied, "but he is most insistent. He said he is here on the King's business and must have a word with you. It's about a runner who disappeared from the Rose and Crown Inn."

"I know nothing of any runner," Mrs. Throckmorton declared with considerable annoyance and glanced around the room. Miss Spencer sat composed, though unnaturally pale. Damaris appeared shocked, and Melody stared at the butler with wide-eyed wonder, while the three gentlemen had risen to their feet. No use in pretending they had not heard . . . Caroline sighed and waved a hand at Wilfred. "Very well, show this man in."

"Very good, Madam." The butler withdrew but was back in a moment and announced in solemn tones, "Mr. Theodore Rumpole."

The runner was a large man with broad shoulders and a barrel chest. He looked to be above forty, but still robust. His hair, once black, was streaked with strands of gray and silver, and his deeply tanned face boasted numerous wrinkles, deepened now by the frown above wide-set blue eyes.

"Thank you for seeing me, Mrs. Throckmorton," he said, addressing the oldest lady in the room. "I apologize for inconveniencing you, but my business is urgent."

"It had best be," Caroline declared. "Or I shall write to the Home Secretary and protest this invasion."

"Yes, ma'am," he replied, his expression revealing none of his thoughts. "Is there somewhere we might speak in private?"

"There is nothing I have to say that cannot be said in front of my family and our friends."

"As you wish, ma'am. I am investigating the disappearance of one John Paul Snelling, a Bow Street Runner who arrived in Chichester on the fourteenth of June and put up at the Rose and Crown Inn. Mr. Snelling was working on his own, investigating a case at the personal request of the Duke of Morcombe, concerning the disappearance of an extremely valuable necklace known as the Sunderland Diamonds."

He paused to observe the reactions of the persons gathered in the room. No one had moved, no one had spoken. The younger ladies regarded him with wide-eyed amazement, and the woman he guessed to be Miss Spencer showed her agitation only by the way her hands twisted a delicate lace handkerchief through her fingers. The faces of the two younger men reflected only curiosity, but the slightly older fellow seemed to avoid his eyes. Interesting, Rumpole thought.

He continued, "Mr. Snelling left behind a journal that contained his notes on the case. His Grace, the Duke of Morcombe, strongly believes that the diamonds were stolen by a distant cousin, one Lady Juliana deVere, who resided in his home until shortly before the theft of the diamonds was noted."

"That is all very well, but I fail to understand what the Sunderland Diamonds have to do with us," Mrs. Throckmorton said, her patience growing thin.

"Please bear with me, ma'am, and it will become clear. Now then, Mr. Snelling traced a young woman he believed to be Lady Juliana to Chichester, and his journal indicates that he had arranged to speak with her privately. That was his last entry."

"I still do not see how this involves anyone in my household," Mrs. Throckmorton declared. "I assure you, no Bow Street Runner called here at any time, or I would know about it."

"Mr. Snelling described the young woman as being of moderate height, slender of build, and with dark auburn hair and blue-green eyes. She is three-and-twenty and—"

"Enough," Juliana said quietly as she rose to her feet. "I believe it is apparent that I am the person you are seeking."

Charles and Oliver immediately closed ranks to stand protectively beside her.

Rumpole gazed at her, then glanced at his notes. "I apprehend you are Miss Juliana Spencer?"

"I am," she said, glad that her long skirt hid her trembling knees.

"I must ask you, Miss Spencer, if you saw or spoke to Mr. Snelling on the fourteenth of June? Of if you—"

"I find this preposterous," Charles interrupted. "Just because Miss Spencer bears a resemblance to the woman you are seeking is hardly sufficient reason to believe she would know anything of this man's disappearance."

Rumpole's gaze raked over him. "And, you sir, are?"

"Charles Harrington, secretary to the Earl of Dysart. Miss Spencer is a particular friend of his lordship's, and I must tell you, sir, he will be most distressed to learn she has been questioned in this manner."

Rumpole's brows rose. "Thank you, Mr. Harrington, I shall bear that in mind. Now, Miss Spencer—"

"I must agree with Harrington," Oliver said, stepping forward. "Miss Spencer has been employed here for the past year, and her character is above reproach. To question her is absurd."

Rumpole sighed. "You are?"

"Oliver Throckmorton. Blandings is my home."

"Then I must thank you for your hospitality, and your . . . er, opinion. I shall take it under advisement." He paused, eyeing the other gentleman in the room speculatively. "Before I continue, is there something you wish to say, sir?"

Geoffrey Evans flushed as everyone turned toward him. "No, sir."

"Then perhaps we might—"

"Except that Miss Spencer is most highly thought of by the vicar," Evans hastily interrupted as he felt Melody's tiny fist pummeling his side. "I am his curate, and although I have been in Chichester only a short time, I have heard Miss Spencer spoken of as a . . . a most virtuous lady."

Rumpole nodded, then glanced at Juliana. "It appears you are extremely fortunate in your friends, Miss Spencer. However, despite these moving testimonials, I must still ask if you saw or spoke to Mr. Snelling."

She could not answer. She stared dumbfounded at the windows, where Faustus now stood, a crumpled black beaver hat dangling from his mouth.

Melody saw her dog at the same instant. "Oh, good heavens, what has he found now? Faustus, come here."

Annoyed, Rumpole turned to glare at the dog. He was about to demand a private interview with Miss Spencer, when something about the hat the animal carried caught his attention.

"Faustus, come here," Melody demanded again. The sheepdog hesitated, then unerringly headed for the group of gentlemen surrounding Miss Spencer. He deposited the crumpled, battered beaver hat, with dirt from the rose garden still clinging to its brim, on the carpet in front of Rumpole.

Mrs. Throckmorton rang for a footman. "I shall have Henry remove that abomination. Melody, my dear, you must—"

"One moment, ma'am," Rumpole said as he knelt to examine the item. When he looked up, his eyes were

163

grave. "Unless I am much mistaken, this is Mr. Snelling's hat."

Charles had turned pale, but he made a valiant effort, knowing his lordship would expect it of him. "Surely one hat is much the same as another? How can you be certain that beaver belonged to Snelling?"

Rumpole withdrew a slightly tarnished spade guinea and held it up so the gold coin caught the light. "Snelling kept this in his hatband in case of an emergency. I think there can be little doubt this hat belonged to him. The question, Mr. Harrington, is where did it come from?"

Charles stared helplessly at the condemning coin, but Melody murmured, "How astonishing. I cannot imagine how it came to be in our gardens, but that must be where Faustus found it, for he had not been out long."

"Then I think I had best have a look at this garden. Mr. Harrington, will you please accompany me? I must ask that no one else leave the house."

Mrs. Throckmorton leaned her head against the back of the chair. "I feel faint," she moaned.

"I shall fetch your smelling salts, Aunt Caroline," Damaris said and hurried from the room.

Juliana felt faint herself and sank into the tall wing chair. There was no help for it now. She would have to confess everything to Mr. Rumpole and plead for mercy. She knew the inquisition she was about to face was no more than what she deserved. Her dishonesty had only made matters worse. She should never have allowed Lord Dysart to conceal the body. . . .

Rumpole returned to the room. His blue eyes had turned to ice and he looked as though he would like to guillotine each of them. "I have found Mr. Snelling," he announced. Focusing on Oliver, he asked with ominous calm, "Mr. Throckmorton, your gardener was just on his way in here to inform you that he'd unearthed a body. What do you know about this?"

"Why, nothing," Oliver declared indignantly. "I never saw or spoke to a Bow Street Runner in my life—excepting you, of course."

"Do not dare accuse my son of any wrongdoing," Mrs. Throckmorton warned, sitting up in her chair. "No woman ever had a finer son or a more honorable one. You might just as well accuse me."

Rumpole, his face inscrutable, nodded. "I shall have to question everyone here. Now if you people will—," he broke off as his gaze swept the room. "Where's the other young lady?"

"If you are referring to my niece, Damaris went to fetch my smelling salts. You may be accustomed to finding bodies in your garden, but I find the experience extraordinarily unsettling."

"Have someone find her, if you please."

Caroline was about to argue further, but Oliver placed a hand on her shoulder. "I believe it best if we oblige Mr. Rumpole, Mama. The sooner he speaks to everyone, the sooner he will leave."

Melody volunteered to find out what was keeping Damaris and hurriedly left, but she was back within moments. She stood in the doorway, her heart-shaped face abnormally pale, her brown eyes wide with concern. "She's not in the house, Mama. Margie said she came up to her bedchamber, then left with her pelisse and reticule. Where can she have gone?"

Mrs. Throckmorton rose from her chair and clutched her bosom. "That unnatural girl has gone to him, I know it. Mrs. Fitzhugh warned me how it would be, but I would not listen, and now . . . oh, was anyone ever so wretchedly taken in? I shall never, never forgive her!"

"Where is it you think the girl has gone?" Rumpole asked.

But no one heard him, as Charles said furiously, "If you are referring to Andrew Marling, I do not believe it. Miss Montague had every opportunity to speak with him, and she declined to do so. I assure you, she wants nothing to do with him."

"Who is Marling?" Rumpole demanded.

Melody assisted her mother to sit down again, saying persuasively, "I cannot believe Damaris would do such a thing, Mama."

"If you would like me to pray?" Geoffrey Evans offered, but only Melody paid him any heed.

"I agree with Charles, Mama," Oliver said. "Damaris finally realized the sort of cad Marling is. She refused to speak with him at Cressy's."

"There must be some other explanation," Juliana said as she went to her employer and poured Mrs. Throckmorton a fresh cup of tea. And, with a hope of her own, added, "Perhaps she went to find Lord Dysart."

"And what has his lordship to do with this?" Rumpole demanded. When he was ignored, he strode to the windows and beckoned to the gardener. "Stay beside the body and see that no one touches it until I return, understood?" As the gardener nodded, Rumpole turned to face the room. They were all crowded around Mrs. Throckmorton and talking two to a dozen. He pursed his lips and let loose a shrill whistle.

When the stunned group looked around at him, he roared, "There has been a murder in this house, and I want some answers. You, sir," he said, pointing at Oliver, "will answer me, and I don't want to hear a word from anyone else. Now then, who is this young lady that disappeared?"

"My cousin, Miss Damaris Montague."

166

"And where is it your mother thinks she's gone?"

Mrs. Throckmorton's breast heaved. "To that fortune hunter. If you are truly from Bow Street, you should go after her—"

"Please, ma'am, allow your son to speak. I shall try to find your niece, but I will be able to do so a great deal faster if I can obtain some plain answers. Now then, sir?"

"My cousin is a considerable heiress, and a gentleman reputed to be a fortune hunter followed her here from London. He is putting up at the Rose and Crown Inn, and my mother fears Damaris may have gone to him."

"His name, sir?"

"Andrew Marling, but I have to tell you, Mr. Rumpole, I do not agree with my mother. My cousin did, for a time, show an interest in Marling, but not recently. For the past few days, she has taken pains to avoid him. I cannot believe she went to him willingly, but he may have contrived to somehow lure her away or kidnap her."

"Very well. 'Tis clear I'll get no sense of any of you until Miss Montague is found. I am going to the Rose and Crown. If this chit is there, I will find her and bring her back here." He eyed them with a baleful glare, and warned, "In the meantime I am ordering you, with the authority vested in me by the Magistrate's Court, not to leave this house."

Mr. Evans stepped forward. "I beg your pardon, but I must return to the vicarage. I have duties—"

"I said no one is to leave, and unless you wish to be taken up on charges, you will remain here. Is that quite clear?"

Theodore Rumpole was an intelligent man, and he had solved a number of cases for the Bow Street Magistrate's

Court, but seldom had he encountered a more difficult group of people to interrogate than the household at Blandings. It was with considerable relief that he climbed into his carriage, lit a cigar, and ordered his driver to take him to the inn.

He had questioned the proprietor, Abel Jones, earlier in the day. Short, grossly fat, and slovenly, the innkeeper had inherited the Rose and Crown from his wife's father and, from what Rumpole could gather, spent more of his time in the taproom than seeing to the running of the place. It was his wife, a dour, blunt-spoken woman, who saw to the guests.

This time Rumpole made inquiries of one of the postboys, then went straight to the kitchen, where Mrs. Jones was overseeing the dinner with the help of a couple of scullery maids. She was not pleased to have her preparations interrupted, or impressed with his credentials. She told him he would either have to question her while she worked or wait until dinner was served.

"I shall try to be brief," Rumpole promised her. "But I need to know what you can tell me about one of your guests—Mr. Andrew Marling."

Her long, thin face radiated contempt. "Good riddance to bad rubbish," she muttered, plunking a freshly plucked fowl down on the plank table. "If it's him you be wanting, you'd best make haste. He packed his bags and left not more 'an twenty minutes past, and if I'd not been on the watch, he would have bolted without paying his shot."

"Did he have anyone with him? A young lady, perhaps?"

She picked up a heavy cleaver and with deft strokes dismembered the bird. "A girl came in, demanding to see 'im, an' if it had been me, I would've sent her on her way. It ain't decent, coming to an inn to see a man, and her all alone. But Mr. Jones was out front, and he's a soft heart for a pretty lass, and there she was, crying like there'd be no tomorrow if she didn't get to see Marling."

"Did she leave with him?"

"Mayhap she meant to fly with him, but Lord Dysart put a stop to that quick enough."

"Dysart," Rumpole murmured. "What business did his lordship have here?"

The woman's brows rose as she used the cleaver to shove the sliced chicken aside and placed a fresh one on the table. "His lordship don't rightly confide in me, but it were him what sent Marling on his way. That hoity-toity Londoner thought he was better an' most, but Lord Dysart made short work of 'im." She sighed, pausing in her chopping for a moment. "A right pleasure to watch, it was."

"I see, and the young lady? Where is Miss Montague now?"

Mrs. Jones shrugged her bony shoulders. "Now, 'ow would I be knowing that? All I can tell you is that his lordship took her off with him. Like as not, he went home."

Rumpole, his brow furrowed, thanked her, then walked slowly out to his carriage. He didn't want to chase Lord Dysart about the countryside, though he suspicioned he would have to interrogate the earl before the case was done. For now, he hoped that assuring Mrs. Throckmorton that her niece had not eloped with Marling would be sufficient. It was not his business to be chasing a runaway heiress, though he had a strong feeling Mrs. Throckmorton would not agree. Reluctantly, he ordered his driver to take him back to Blandings.

His foreboding was correct. The instant he stepped

foot in the drawing room, Mrs. Throckmorton was on him like a tick on a dog.

"Did you find her? Tell me the worst—'tis true, she has eloped with Marling? Oh, that wretched, wretched girl!"

Rumpole held a hand up. "Pray calm yourself, ma'am. Your niece may have intended to fly to Gretna Green, but she did not—leastwise not with Marling."

"Then where is she?"

"From what I could discover, she went off with Lord Dysart."

His announcement caused a new outburst of pandemonium, and it was several moments before Rumpole could make himself heard. He ordered everyone to be seated, and when quiet was restored, he stated, "I do not wish to inconvenience you longer than necessary, ma'am, but there is a dead runner buried in your garden, and I must and will have answers. I want to know how that body came to be there. Now then, Miss Spencer, once again, did you see Mr. Snelling?"

Charles Harrington rose nobly to his feet. "I am the one you need to question, sir. I buried Snelling."

Amid the uproar that ensued, Lord Dysart quietly entered the drawing room, followed by two other people. Only Rumpole, who faced the door, noticed his entrance.

Dysart listened for a moment, his gaze drawn to Juliana, who was staring transfixed at Charles. She appeared drawn, the shadows under her eyes more marked than when he'd left, but he drank in the sight of her as hungrily as a man dying of thirst.

As if sensing his regard, Juliana turned toward the door and gasped.

Dysart stepped forward. "Thank you, Charles. Your loyalty is most commendable, but it never pays to lie to Bow Street. 'Tis time the truth of this matter was revealed." He turned to the pair behind him, urging them forward. "Miss Montague, I suggest you join your aunt."

The other gentleman who had come in with Dysart scowled furiously as his lordship said to the room in general, "May I introduce to you His Grace, the Duke of Morcombe."

Chapter 12

Oblivious to the others, Juliana stood transfixed, staring at her cousin Lucian. It had been two years since she had seen him, but he had changed little. The cold gray eyes beneath pale, nearly colorless brows raked over her. She could almost touch the wave of hatred that emanated from those eyes. He would harm her if he could.

Repulsed, she took a step back and her gaze shifted to Dysart. How could he have betrayed her so? To think that she had prayed for his return, counted the hours and the minutes, only to have him appear with the one man in the world she had hoped never to see again. She had felt disaster was impending when the runner had written her, and dismayed that her small world was crumbling beneath her feet when she'd discovered Snelling dead—but that was nothing compared to the utter misery that filled her heart now. She closed her eyes briefly, unable to bear to look into the dark eyes she had once trusted implicitly.

Dysart spoke, the deep melodious voice she had so missed cutting through her like a knife. "His Grace has something he wishes to say."

Rumpole held up a hand. "I assume, sir, that you are Lord Dysart? I am exceedingly grateful to you for bringing Miss Montague home, and I shall have some questions to put to both you and His Grace, but at the moment I am conducting an investigation into the murder of a Bow Street Runner."

"Which is why I am here," Dysart replied with easy cordiality. "Bear with me, please. I think you will find what His Grace has to say most interesting."

"This is most irregular—," Rumpole began.

Mrs. Throckmorton plied her fan. "Perhaps we should offer His Grace some refreshments. . . . He will think us quite inhospitable. Melody, my dear, ring for Emily."

Charles drew Damaris into the alcove near the window. "Why did you leave, my dear? I have been near mad with worry. Your aunt would have it that you meant to elope with Marling, but that I could not accept. . . ."

"I had no choice," she murmured, tears again brimming her eyes.

Across the room, Oliver whispered to his sister, "I cannot say I like the look of His Grace. And what can he have to do with that man buried in the garden?"

Contempt curling his lip, the duke glared at them all, then addressed Juliana, his voice carrying easily across the small room. "You left Morcombe for this? Really, my dear cousin, I had thought you possessed of better taste."

Mrs. Throckmorton beamed with satisfaction and remarked to her daughter, "There! Did I not always say Miss Spencer was a true lady? Cousin to a duke. Only wait until Mrs. Fitzhugh hears . . . but I wonder why she never said."

"I doubt I would claim him, either," Oliver replied, having taken an instant dislike to His Grace.

As the hum of voices rose, Rumpole prayed someone would deliver him from this bedlam he'd wandered into. He detested cases involving the peerage. It was always the same—they had scant respect for the law. And it was no use protesting. Gentlemen like Lord Dysart were too accustomed to having their own way. He felt a small tug on his sleeve and turned to find Miss Throckmorton regarding him timidly.

"Would you care for a cup of tea, Mr. Rumpole?"

173

Tea! This investigation was turning into a blooming tea party! He waved her away as the Duke of Morcombe started to speak.

"I came here to apologize to my cousin, Lady Juliana," His Grace said, sounding as though the words were forced from his throat. The room quieted instantly. "Two years ago, just after she left Morcombe, I discovered a priceless necklace was missing. The piece, known as the Sunderland Diamonds, had been in the deVere family for hundreds of years. I . . . I mistakenly assumed Lady Juliana had taken the necklace, and laid information with Bow Street. Subsequently, a runner was engaged to find the lady. However, the necklace was merely mislaid, and I have sent word to Bow Street withdrawing all charges against Lady Juliana. That is all I came to say."

Anything less like an apology Rumpole had never heard. He rose as the duke turned to leave. "Just a moment, Your Grace."

The aquiline features lifted haughtily. "Are you addressing me?" He glanced at Dysart. "Who is this man?"

"I am Theodore Rumpole from the Bow Street Magistrate's Court. I was sent here to investigate the disappearance of John Paul Snelling—the runner you engaged to find Lady Juliana—who unfortunately has turned up dead. Murdered and buried in the garden here. Now then, I have a few questions."

"I suggest you direct them to Lady Juliana. I have not seen nor heard from any runner in over six months."

"He didn't write to you and inform you that he had found Lady Juliana, that she was, in fact, engaged as a governess here and using the name Miss Spencer?"

"He most emphatically did not."

Rumpole turned his tired gaze on Juliana. "Miss Spencer, uh Lady Juliana, I am going to ask you once more—did you talk to Mr. Snelling?"

She still stood near the windows, but now Lord Dysart stood next to her, and somehow his hand was clasping hers. The knowledge that he had not betrayed her, that he had somehow forced Lucian to admit he'd falsely accused her, filled her with an undeniable joy. Even if Rumpole arrested her for Snelling's murder, she would still have this moment to remember.

She lifted her chin slightly and replied honestly, "Yes, I did. Mr. Snelling came to the house late on the evening of the sixteenth. I spoke with him in the library."

"The sixteenth," Mrs. Throckmorton murmured. "Why, that was the night of the ball. Do you mean to tell me—"

"Please, ma'am," Rumpole interrupted. "Allow me to ask the questions. Now then, Lady Juliana, will you tell me why Snelling approached you? His orders were merely to find you and notify His Grace."

"Apparently Mr. Snelling did not care for my cousin," she said, glancing disdainfully at Lucian. "Your runner offered to betray His Grace and keep my whereabouts a secret . . . for the sum of fifty pounds. He said he would return the following week at midnight for my answer."

Now they were getting somewhere, Rumpole thought, but he was disheartened that a runner had resorted to what was little better than blackmail. Hiding his feelings, he asked, "And what was your answer, Lady Juliana? Did you see Snelling again? Did you pay him?"

"No, Mr. Rumpole. I intended to, but when I came down to the library, I found someone had . . . had hit Mr. Snelling over the head with a small statue. I believed then, and still believe, that my cousin somehow found out the runner meant to double-cross him and it was he who murdered Snelling."

"How utterly preposterous," the duke drawled. "I have not left my home in over a year, and I have witnesses to prove it. Surely it should be obvious that Lady Juliana

175

struck the runner down herself to prevent his blackmailing her, then buried the body. I demand you do your duty, Rumpole, and arrest her."

Dysart, his eyes dark with fury, glared at Lucian. "I suggest, Your Grace, that unless you wish to meet me on the dueling field, you refrain from making any further allegations against Lady Juliana. I assure you, it would give me considerable pleasure to run you through."

"Your devotion to my cousin is rather touching, Dysart, if somewhat misguided. But I can understand it. Did she tell you that I once offered to wed her? Of course, that was before I learned she could not be trusted—"

"You cur!" Dysart lunged forward, but Rumpole stepped between him and the duke.

"Enough, the pair of you. Need I remind you that dueling is against the law? If you do not restrain yourselves, I shall have you both brought up on charges."

"I think you forget to whom you are speaking," Lucian warned.

"No, Your Grace, but you are not above the law, and I am here by the King's authority to solve a murder, and I fully intend to do so." He paused, glancing around the room. Satisfied that, at least for the moment, there would be no further interference, he turned to Lady Juliana again. "What did you do when you discovered that Snelling was dead?"

She felt Dysart's hand squeezing her own. Drawing a deep breath, she confessed, "I was badly frightened. . . . I know it was foolish of me, but I left Mr. Snelling as I had found him and returned to my room."

Rumpole's mouth dropped open. "Are you telling me, Lady Juliana, that you found a dead man in the library and instead of rousing the house, you just went calmly to bed?"

"Not . . . not calmly. I was very distraught, and I suppose I was not thinking clearly. I had hoped that if no one knew Mr. Snelling had come to see me, then I need not be involved. I knew my cousin had laid false charges against me, and though I was innocent of Snelling's death, I feared I would be arrested for stealing the Sunderland Diamonds. . . . It was cowardly of me, and wrong, but I swear to you, Mr. Rumpole, I had nothing to do with the runner's death."

Against his will, he believed her. Sighing, he asked, "And the next morning? Who discovered the body?"

"No one," Juliana said simply. "When the maid woke me, all was as usual. I dressed and came belowstairs, expecting at any moment to hear a cry of alarm. I waited until after breakfast, then looked into the library. Snelling's body had disappeared."

Rumpole ran a hand through his gray hair. This was the most bizarre case he'd come across. If he had his choice, he would lock Lady Juliana and her cousin up, and maybe Lord Dysart, too, until he got some reasonable answers. He glared at the occupants of the room, but for once no one was saying a word. The sheepdog, lying now next to the earl, seemed to sense the tension in the air and whimpered.

Melody half rose to see to Faustus, but as Rumpole's head swiveled in her direction, she hastily sat down again.

The door opened and the butler stepped tentatively into the room.

"What is it, now?" Rumpole demanded.

Wilfred, ignoring him, addressed Mrs. Throckmorton. "Dinner is served, Madam."

"No one is going to dinner or anywhere else until I get to the bottom of this affair," Rumpole roared as he strode toward the butler. Wilfred hastily retreated, and the man from Bow Street slammed the door shut.

Turning, he glared at the occupants of the room, then

suddenly pointed a finger at Harrington. "You, sir. You said earlier that you had buried Snelling. How did you get drawn into this affair?"

Dysart cleared his throat. "I do not mean to interfere, Rumpole, but—"

"Then don't."

"The thing is, Mr. Harrington did not bury the body. When he said he did so, he was only trying to protect Lady Juliana, and me."

"And how do you know that, sir?"

"Because I am the one who buried Snelling."

Charles looked gratefully at his employer, while Damaris, sitting beside him, gasped aloud. Melody stared at the earl in awe, and Mrs. Throckmorton had recourse to her smelling salts. Geoffrey Evans prayed fervently and wiped his brow with his handkerchief. Oliver sat stunned, wondering how he could have missed so much happening right beneath his nose.

Rumpole muttered a pungent oath under his breath and entertained serious thoughts of retirement.

His Grace, lounging in a tall wing chair, smiled maliciously. "How very chivalrous. She bashed him over the head, and you concealed the body."

Dysart appealed to Rumpole. "If you will allow me to explain?"

"By all means, my lord, I should dearly appreciate a rational explanation from someone."

"Although Lady Juliana did not know it, I had overheard her first conversation with Snelling. Knowing that she was to meet him again, I planned to be on hand in case she had need of me—"

"Which she obviously did," Lucian murmured.

Ignoring him, Dysart held the rest of his audience spellbound as he continued, "It had rained heavily that night, and I was a few moments late arriving. When I came up on the terrace, I thought I heard someone mak-

178

ing off in the night. At first, I assumed it was Snelling. Then, I saw Lady Juliana kneeling beside the body. . . ," he hesitated but, knowing it had to be said, continued softly, "When I realized Snelling was dead, I thought Lady Juliana had taken fright and defended herself against him."

"A perfectly logical assumption," Lucian said.

"I also knew her cousin had falsely accused of her taking the Sunderland Diamonds and that she feared him too much to even attempt to clear her name. It's true I moved the body and buried it, but only to ensure that I had sufficient time to prove Lady Juliana's innocence—both of stealing the diamonds and of murdering Snelling."

"You realize that you have aided and abetted a murderer?" Rumpole said, but his voice lacked conviction.

"No sir, not a murderer. If Lady Juliana was responsible for Snelling's death, it had to have been in self-defense. Of course, I know now that she had nothing to do with it."

"This is absurd," Lucian fumed. "She killed him, and Dysart got rid of the body. What more do you need, Rumpole?"

"Lady Juliana was not responsible for Snelling's death," Dysart repeated as he walked slowly across the room. "Someone else was on the terrace that night, and much as I hate to admit it, I know it was not His Grace." He paused before Damaris. Reaching down, he took her hand and gently drew her up to stand beside him. "I believe Miss Montague may shed some light on this mystery."

The color drained from Damaris's face as the attention of everyone in the room focused on her.

Charles rose to his feet beside her and angrily faced his employer. "You cannot be serious, my lord. I know you have not always thought highly of Miss Montague, but surely you do not believe her capable of murder?"

Ignoring his secretary, Dysart said to Damaris, "Marling told me everything. I swear you have nothing to fear, but you must tell the truth now."

Damaris, her large green eyes filling with tears, turned to Charles. Looking up at him, her eyes begging him to understand, she said, "I am so sorry. . . . I told you I had met Andrew secretly."

Biting her lip, she turned to Dysart. "I thought Andrew . . . I thought he cared for me, and we had planned to elope that night. I crept down to the library. He had promised to meet me on the terrace, but as I approached the windows, a large man suddenly stepped inside. I was frightened. I thought he was a burglar, and I grabbed a small statue that is kept on a stand there and hit him. You must believe me—I only meant to . . . to stop him from coming into the house."

"Go on," Rumpole encouraged the girl. Finally someone was admitting to something.

"I was scared, and I ran outside to find Andrew . . . only he had not come. It had stormed badly that evening, and I learned later that his carriage had lost a wheel when it hit a rut in the road."

"Did you tell Marling what you had done?" Rumpole asked.

She nodded tearfully. "The next day. When I told him what happened, he wanted me to fly with him. But I was afraid that when the body was discovered, there would be a hue and cry, and if we were missing the Runners would come after us."

Rumpole consulted his notes. "I see. Now then, you fled to the terrace after hitting Snelling, but this Marling was not there. Did you see anyone else about?"

Her head down, she said barely loud enough for him to hear, "Not then. I went back inside and I was in the hall when Miss Spencer came down. I waited until she went into the library, then ran up to my bedchamber."

Rumpole sighed heavily. "I find it extraordinary that two young ladies find a dead body, and neither thinks to rouse the household."

Damaris glanced up at him, her large eyes glistening with tears, her tiny chin quavering. "Are you going to . . . arrest me?"

"Of course he is not," Charles said, sending a look in the agent's direction that dared him to try it.

Oliver, coming up on her other side, placed a comforting arm about her shoulders. "You may be a scatterbrained peagoose, Cousin, but I think it's obvious Snelling's death was an accident—and his own fault. If he had not tried to blackmail Miss Spencer, nothing would have happened to him."

Damaris turned to Juliana. "Can you forgive me, Miss Spencer—I mean, Lady Juliana? I never thought that they would accuse you, but I left a letter for Aunt Caroline explaining what had occurred—"

"This is all quite touching, but most tedious," Lucian said as he rose. "Since this . . . person has admitted to murdering your runner, I trust my presence is no longer needed? Juliana, my dear, such a pleasure to see you again, but I really must take my leave. I have been away from Morcombe too long as—," he broke off as the earl strode toward him. "Pray do not disturb yourself, Dysart. I can find my way out."

"I wish to be certain you are indeed gone," his lordship replied as he opened the door for the duke. "And if I ever see you anywhere near Lady Juliana, or hear you have so much as spoken her name, I promise you will regret it."

"That sounds suspiciously like a threat."

"It is," Dysart agreed as they stepped into the hall.

"Now then," Rumpole began, but he broke off and swung around as Melody cried out in alarm. "What the devil's wrong now, miss?"

"It is Mama! Oh, Oliver, she has fainted!"

Mrs. Throckmorton's chin rested against her chest in an unbecoming manner. One arm hung limply over the edge of a chair, and a teacup lay on the carpet where she'd apparently dropped it.

Juliana hurried to her employer's side. Kneeling next to the chair, she opened a small vial of ammonia water and waved it beneath Mrs. Throckmorton's nose. Melody knelt on the other side of her mother, taking her lifeless hand in her own and rubbing it briskly. Damaris, Charles, and Geoffrey Evans crowded around, offering advice and suggestions.

Behind them, Rumpole groaned. This case was never going to get sorted out.

As Mrs. Throckmorton's eyes slowly fluttered open and she moaned softly, Melody appealed to Rumpole. "Please, sir, may I take Mama up to her bedchamber?"

"I suppose that would be best. 'Tis obvious neither of you were involved in Snelling's death, but all the same, I want your word that you will not leave the house."

Melody nodded, then returned to her mother's side. She knelt by the chair and said softly, "If you can manage to walk, Mama, I will help you up to your room. I am sure you will feel much better once you rest awhile."

Mrs. Throckmorton, however, refused to leave. She told Melody to bring her a glass of sherry, then glanced at Rumpole. "Pray do not let me distract you, sir. No doubt I fainted merely because I have not had a bite to eat since breakfast. Not that I mean to criticize you, Mr. Rumpole. I am very sure anyone in your position would not think twice about ordering dinner set back, and although those of us who suffer from indifferent health may find it taxing, we would not for a moment dream of impeding your investigation."

Rumpole stared speechlessly. He had seen Mrs. Throckmorton consume the better part of a dish of macaroons and a number of scones that had been brought in with the tea.

The lady of the house sipped her sherry, then glanced up at him. "There, that is most reviving, but I am wondering if we might not have a plate of sandwiches made up and brought in? Surely that would not disturb you? But I am forgetting my manners. Would you care for a fresh cup of tea, or perhaps something stronger? We have brandy or scotch, port. . . . You may ask Oliver for whatever you wish. Of course, I do not normally imbibe at this hour, but it has after all been a most exceptional day, and Dr. Girard has frequently advised that an occasional glass can be quite beneficial to the constitution."

"Thank you, ma'am, and I may request something later, but first I must arrange to have Mr. Snelling's body removed, and then statements must be taken from Lord Dysart, Lady Juliana, and Miss Montague. However, if I may impose on your hospitality, a sandwich would not go amiss."

"Of course. But Mr. Rumpole, if you are hungry, then may I suggest that you postpone your reports until later and allow us all to sit down to a decent meal? It will be no trouble to lay another place, and I am sure you will find matters will go much more smoothly when everyone is not preoccupied with thoughts of roast venison or Chicken Marengo. 'Tis so difficult for one to think clearly when one is famished."

Whether it was thoughts of the venison or merely the realization that he would accomplish nothing until Mrs. Throckmorton was properly fed, Rumpole capitulated but added sternly, "However, as soon as we have dined, I must insist on interviewing Miss Montague, Lady Juliana, and Lord Dysart in a private room—and without interruptions."

"It shall be arranged, only . . . oh dear, I hope you will not take offense, but I must tell you, sir, that I cannot help but think it improper for you to speak to my niece or Lady Juliana alone."

"Improper!" Rumpole exploded. "Ma'am, may I remind you that both of these young ladies were involved in the murder of a Bow Street Runner? That both of these young ladies behaved most improperly in meeting gentlemen alone at midnight, that one of them intended to fly to Gretna Green, and the other was being blackmailed?"

She stared up at him, puzzled. "But, Mr. Rumpole, you must see that I did not *know* my niece intended to meet that scoundrel Marling. Had I known, I would certainly never have permitted it. As for Lady Juliana, while she is not related to me and although I cannot forbid such conduct, I naturally would have advised against it."

Oliver grinned sympathetically at Rumpole. Aloud he suggested, "I am sure that if one of the maids were stationed in the room, that would satisfy the proprieties. Is that agreeable to you, Rumpole?"

The investigator nodded. He didn't know why anyone bothered to ask him, since his wishes were consistently ignored, but anything to get this case over and done with. Then he would definitely consider retiring.

"Excellent," Mrs. Throckmorton approved. "Melody, my dear, ring for Emily. We must let Cook know there will be . . . ," she paused to look around, mentally counting the faces. "Mr. Evans, the hour is late, and I am certain they have already dined at the vicarage. Will you stay for dinner?"

Considering that his stomach had been growling for a quarter hour, and knowing he would get a much better meal at Blandings, he would have agreed even if Melody had not looked so hopefully at him. "I would be grateful, Mrs. Throckmorton, but I must send a message explaining my delay."

"Yes, naturally. Melody will arrange it." She counted noses and was about to dispatch the maid to the kitchen when Lord Dysart returned. She immediately extended an invitation to him as well.

His lordship hesitated, glancing at Rumpole.

The investigator shrugged. "You may as well, my lord. I have been persuaded to let the reports wait until my appetite has been appeased."

"Much the wisest course," Mrs. Throckmorton added, nodding in approval. "Emily, please tell Cook we will sit down nine to dinner. But mind you, gentlemen, I will have no discussion of this business at the table. 'Tis bad for the digestion."

Chapter 13

Juliana expected the cook to walk out in protest. Mrs. Throckmorton's blithe assumption that Jean-Claude would have no problem in increasing the covers to nine was due only to her unfamiliarity with both the chef and the kitchen. Under normal circumstances, Juliana would have gone to the kitchen to personally soothe the Frenchman, but she was still reeling both from the shock of having seen her cousin suddenly appear in the drawing room and from the revelation that Damaris had accidentally killed poor Snelling.

But belowstairs, Jean-Claude was busy rallying the kitchen staff into preparing a meal fit for a duke—or the daughter of one. The news had rapidly spread—from the gardener to the scullery maid to the second cook to Jean-Claude himself—that a dead man had been found in the rose garden. Then the butler had told one of the footmen that a Bow Street Runner had called and was asking questions about Miss Spencer. Emily, who had been in and out of the drawing room, passed along the information that Miss Spencer was really Lady Juliana, the daughter of the former Duke of Morcombe, and that it was Miss Montague who had clanked the Bow Street Runner over the head and Lord Dysart who had buried him near the sundial.

There had not been so much excitement and speculation in the kitchen since Mr. Throckmorton had passed on. Miss Spencer was a favorite among the staff, and Jean-Claude had declared fervently that he was not in the least surprised by the news, for he had always thought her a true lady. In her honor, he brought his genius and ingenuity to bear, managing to prepare a sumptuous meal in little better than half an hour.

Juliana was unaware of the devotion and effort she'd stirred in the kitchen. When dinner was announced the second time that evening, she allowed Lord Dysart to lead her into the dining room, following Oliver and his mother. Mr. Evans escorted Melody, Charles gave his arm to Damaris, and Rumpole was left to bring up the rear. However, he was given a place of honor, seated on the left side of his hostess, while Dysart sat on her right.

Juliana glanced dazedly around the table, unaware of the fond glances of the two footmen who served the meal. Except for the uneven numbers, it appeared much as any other dinner. Under Mrs. Throckmorton's stern gaze, the hum of conversation rose and fell, though it did not touch on any but the most mundane topics. The gentlemen ate heartily, and even Damaris and Melody, with the resiliency of youth, did credit to the chef's superb offerings. Juliana, however, had little appetite.

After two covers were removed with Lady Juliana barely touching her food, Lord Dysart, seated next to her, remarked quietly, "The worst is behind us now. Trust me, my dear, all charges will be dispensed with. You have nothing more to worry you."

She smiled wanly and nibbled at the baby carrots. Lord Dysart might consider all trouble behind him, but her life was quite unsettled. Mrs. Throckmorton had announced plans to take both Melody and Damaris to London for the Season, and it was clear she expected Juliana to accompany them. But judging by the glances exchanged between Charles Harrington and Damaris, her own days as a chaperon were plainly numbered. Nor did she want to go to London.

Of course she could resume using her title now, and she need no longer fear meeting any of her old friends, but Juliana still felt reluctant to face them. She didn't want their pity. She had seen other ladies forced by reduced circumstances to seek employment. Their old acquaintances were kind and meant well, but one could not mistake the sympathetic looks, the air of gentle concern, the murmurs of, "Oh, my dear, if I hear of a suitable position. . . ."

If she had an income that would allow her to move in the first circles as she once had done, it would be different. But despite the title, despite her lineage, she was as far removed from London's social whirl as was Jean-Claude in the kitchen. Further, perhaps. At least his culinary skill would be admired and appreciated, while she had nothing to offer except her rather dubious talent as a governess and companion. Even in that, she thought, she had failed miserably, or Damaris would not have been secretly planning to elope.

Mistaking Juliana's quiet and listlessness, Lord Dysart asked, "Are you angry that I brought your cousin here? I know you had no desire to see him, but I feared it was the only way to persuade Bow Street to dismiss the charges he laid against you."

"Angry? Indeed not. I own I was . . . surprised at first, but you must believe that I am deeply grateful to you, my lord, although I cannot imagine how you managed to persuade him to come with you."

Dysart laughed. "I shall tell you later. 'Tis a topic I doubt Mrs. Throckmorton would wish to hear discussed at her table, but I can promise you that you will never be troubled by him again."

"I still cannot entirely comprehend it," Juliana said,

shaking her head. "I never believed Lucian would admit that the charges were false."

"Well, he has done so now, my dear, and we can all return to some semblance of normalcy. Which reminds me, a letter from Maman was waiting for me when I returned from Morcombe. She is back in England and most anxious to meet you."

Juliana paled. "You wrote to her about me?"

"Naturally. I explained that you were Philip's little sister. She remembers him with great fondness, and she sends her deepest condolences to you, along with the hope that you will be able to visit soon."

Mrs. Throckmorton demanded his attention, and as Dysart turned away, Juliana recalled the words he'd spoken the night before he left for Morcombe. *When this business is settled, I shall take you to stay with Maman, and then we may all decide what is best for you to do.* Dear Dysart. He still felt responsible for her and determined to see she was creditably established. He believed he owed that much to Philip. Would he, she wondered, try to find a husband for her? It would be a futile effort, but she could not tell him that. Nor could she visit his mother, who would undoubtedly see in a moment that Juliana was in love with her son.

Mr. Evans, seated on Juliana's left, remarked with a pleased sigh, "I cannot think when I have enjoyed a better meal. Mrs. Throckmorton is certainly blessed to have such a cook in her employ."

"Indeed, sir," she replied, managing a smile for Henry as he removed her plate, "all of the staff at Blandings are excellent."

"It has been a most unusual day, but I cannot be sorry that Mr. Rumpole insisted I stay. Such a dinner—not that I mean to complain about the meals at the vicarage, but there can be no comparison. I fear I am tempted to spend more time at Blandings than I ought."

Setting aside her own dreary thoughts, Juliana smiled. "Because of the dinners, sir? I rather thought a certain young lady had drawn you to the house."

He blushed furiously and stole a quick look at Melody, seated on the opposite side of the table. She was engaged in conversation with Rumpole, but as if sensing his gaze, she turned her head and smiled blindingly at Evans.

Another match in the making, Juliana thought, envying Melody. She was rather young yet, but her affections, once formed, were steadfast, and Geoffrey Evans seemed patently right for her. It was not the alliance Mrs. Throckmorton had hoped for, but in another year or so, she would undoubtedly allow the betrothal.

Mrs. Throckmorton rose, signaling it was time the ladies withdrew. She had arranged for Mr. Rumpole to make use of the library, and he would interview Lord Dysart first. The rest of the gentlemen would remain in the dining room, enjoying their brandy and cigars, while the ladies retired to the drawing room. Rumpole would send for Lady Juliana, then Damaris, and Emily would be positioned at the door for the sake of propriety.

"Now then," Rumpole said, frowning sternly at Lord Dysart after his lordship had taken him through the facts of the case once more. "The court will take a dim view of your moving the body. I understand your reasons, but nevertheless, it was highly improper. There may well be some sort of sanction levied against you, my lord, though I shall certainly mention that it was through your efforts that the case was solved."

"I would much prefer you omitted any mention of me," Dysart replied lazily.

"Are you trying to bribe me, sir?"

"No, not at all, though I am doing what I can to assist you. Think how much more impressive it would look on

190

your record if you had solved the case—which I am very sure you would have done, given more time."

Rumpole, incurably honest, replied dryly, "Thank you, my lord, but I am not as certain. It seemed to me that Lady Juliana must be the culprit. Tell me, how did you guess it was Miss Montague?"

"Confidentially?" Dysart asked. When the investigator agreed, he replied, "It was happenstance. The morning after I moved the body, I tried to discuss the affair with Lady Juliana, but I could not manage more than a few minutes alone with her. I suggested she meet me on the terrace at midnight, which I must tell you she was most reluctant to do. However, I prevailed. It was the only way I could think of to speak with her privately—but even then we werc interrupted."

"By Miss Montague?"

Dysart nodded. "I rather thought I heard someone else on the far end of the terrace, but when I went to see, Miss Montague stepped out of the darkness and prevented me from chasing the intruder. She claimed she had come down because she heard a noise, but I suspected she was meeting someone, and with Andrew Marling in the neighborhood, it wasn't hard to figure out who."

"I wonder it did not occur to you, at that point, to call in Bow Street. The young lady was never in any real danger—it was clearly an accident."

"But I was not thinking of Miss Montague," Dysart said, grinning. "Lady Juliana *was* in danger of being arrested because of the charges her cousin had laid against her. You must see I could not call you in until I had time to clear her name. You said yourself that you were inclined to think her the culprit."

"But you had not talked to Marling before you left for Morcombe. Why were you so certain Lady Juliana was innocent?"

Dysart laughed aloud. "If you had come to know her as

I have, the thought that she could be anything but innocent would never occur to you. I have never met a more honorable person or a lady with more integrity or sense of responsibility than Lady Juliana. Even my mother, a woman of eminent respectability, is not above looking the other way on occasion—"

"A trait obviously inherited by her son."

With an engaging smile, Dysart confided, "Maman's sins are limited to smuggling in a few bottles of brandy when she returns home from France. Mine, until now, involved only baiting the watch when I was younger, and a duel or two that I could not avoid."

Lord Dysart's duels with several irate husbands were common knowledge, and Rumpole said dryly, "So I have heard. Perhaps continued association with Lady Juliana will have a beneficial effect on your conduct. However, I must say that, in this particular instance, you have behaved most chivalrously."

"I rather believe I have," Dysart said. "Which is why I hate to see a report filed that will have the scandalmongers dragging not only my name through the mud, but that of Lady Juliana as well. She deserves better."

Rumpole's eyes narrowed. "What precisely are you suggesting, my lord?"

"Just that any mention of Lady Juliana or myself be omitted from your reports. A slight alteration and—"

"Impossible, my lord."

"Let us not be hasty, Rumpole." Dysart rose and crossed to the center table where the butler had left a tray containing brandy, cigars, and coffee. He poured two generous measures of the brandy into glasses and carried them back to the desk, setting one in front of the investigator. "It can serve no purpose to bring Lady Juliana into this affair. In the last few years, she has lost both her parents and her brother. Her cousin, whom you met earlier this evening, inherited the estate and drove her from her home. She has struggled to survive, hiding her true identity, because of the false charges he brought against her. Do you not think she has suffered sufficiently?"

"Yes, of course, but I must do my duty, and even if I were so inclined, how could I possibly explain Snelling's death without mentioning her?"

"Snelling . . . ," Dysart mused. "He was not precisely a sterling representative of Bow Street, would you say? What a pity it would be if a newspaper like the *Times* were to print a story about how he attempted to blackmail an innocent young lady. I wonder if John Walter is still publishing the paper. . . . We are rather old friends."

"When it comes to double-dealing, Snelling could not hold a candle to you, my lord."

"I am only suggesting that you . . . curtail your report slightly. If, for instance, you said only that Mr. Snelling, while investigating a case, was mistaken for a housebreaker and accidentally dealt a fatal blow. . . ."

Rumpole idly picked up the glass and swirled the brandy. What Lord Dysart proposed was not entirely without merit. The police in general received sufficiently bad press as it was, and to expose that a Bow Street Runner had resorted to blackmail would benefit no one. He supposed he could lay the entire matter before his superior and leave the decision to him, but knowing the way politics influenced the Magistrate's Court, he suspected Lord Dysart's version would prevail.

He sipped the brandy, then glanced up. "I'm making no promises, you understand, but for Lady Juliana's sake, I shall see what can be contrived."

"All I ask is that you try," Dysart replied and lifted his glass in a salute. "To a man of rare intelligence and understanding."

Rumpole waved him away. "Be off with you and send Miss Montague in. I suppose you can have no objection if I take *her* statement?"

"None at all," Dysart replied.

There was little conversation in the blue drawing room as both Damaris and Juliana waited nervously for Mr. Rumpole to summon them. Mr. Evans had come up to say good night, explaining that it was imperative he return to the vicarage, and Melody had walked with him to the door and then, looking rather dewy-eyed, retired to her bedchamber.

Mrs. Throckmorton had ordered a tea tray brought in, and she fussed with the cups, finding a small measure of comfort in the customary ritual of tea before retiring. She felt a trifle guilty and suspected that she was responsible, at least in part, for her niece's present predicament. If she had taken a firmer hand with Damaris from the beginning or listened when Miss Spencer warned her that the girl might be seeing Marling secretly . . . but it was water under the bridge now, and she could only resolve to do better in the future.

"What is taking him so long?" Damaris asked for the third time in a quarter hour.

"I am sure Mr. Rumpole must have a lot of questions," Juliana replied, sounding a great deal more composed than she felt. She hid her own impatience by diligently working at her needlepoint, but she knew the stitches she set would have to be removed tomorrow. Her hands trembled so much, the stitches were uneven, and what should have been a neat row was glaringly askew.

The door opened and Charles Harrington came in with Oliver.

Both looked rather lighthearted, considering the circumstances, and Mrs. Throckmorton glanced at them sharply.

Charles crossed to stand before Damaris and smiled at her encouragingly. "Rumpole is ready to take your statement now, but you need not be nervous. 'Tis a mere formality."

"I thought he would interview Lady Juliana next," Mrs. Throckmorton said.

"That was the original plan," Oliver told her. "But Lord Dysart somehow persuaded Rumpole that there was no need. It is possible that Lady Juliana's name will not be mentioned at all when he files his report."

"Well, that is certainly good news," his mother replied, "but where is his lordship? Is he still with Mr. Rumpole?"

Oliver shook his head. "He has returned to Windward and asked me to make his excuses and convey his apologies. You know he drove through the night, and it has been a long and tiring day. He looked dead on his feet, but he asked me to tell you that, if you permit, he will call tomorrow."

Charles added, "I promised I would remain and fetch him at once if any further problems arose, but I do not anticipate the need. All that remains is for Rumpole to take Miss Montague's statement. With your permission, ma'am, I shall escort her down."

"Very well, but see that Emily is posted by the door," Mrs. Throckmorton instructed. She glanced at her niece's pale face and, feeling a surge of compassion, added, "Damaris, my dear, would you like me to accompany you?"

"Thank you, Aunt Caroline, but I do not think Mr. Rumpole would permit it."

As his mother looked prepared to argue, Oliver advised, "Let her go alone, Mama. Rumpole is being extraordinarily agreeable. If we cooperate with him, I believe we may scrape through this with a minimum of fuss."

Damaris agreed, assured her aunt she would be fine, then bravely laid her hand on Charles Harrington's arm and walked with him to the door. Her quiet dignity was touching, and Mrs. Throckmorton remarked to her son, "I think Damaris will do very well, now."

Juliana, lost in a world of her own, didn't hear her. She wished Lord Dysart had stayed. She had dozens of questions she wanted to ask him. Her mind told her Charles could answer them just as well, but her heart longed for Dysart's presence. Of course he must be near exhausted, and she did not begrudge him his rest, but all the same she could not help longing to see him, if just for a moment. Foolish of her. She knew she might as well get used to doing without Lord Dysart's company.

Oliver settled in a chair next to his mother while he waited for Damaris to return. As she sipped a cup of tea, he observed Lady Juliana. Considering his news, she seemed unaccountably blue, but he suspected he knew what was troubling her. Leaning forward, he told her, "Lord Dysart asked me to tell you that he hopes you will give him the pleasure of driving out with him tomorrow. He said there can be no objection now. . . . I am not quite sure what he meant by that, but he felt certain you would know."

She smiled a little. How many times had she told his lordship that it would be unsuitable for a mere companion to drive with him? Belatedly realizing that Oliver was waiting for a reply, she murmured that it was merely some nonsense on Dysart's part.

Mrs. Throckmorton concealed a yawn. "Gracious, it has been a tiring day. Oliver, do you think Mr. Rumpole will keep Damaris long?"

Charles wondered the same thing. Belowstairs, he paced the hall restlessly. He, too, had some questions he wished to ask Damaris, provided she was not too distressed after giving her statement to Rumpole. It had rocked him on his heels when he learned she had fled to Marling. Charles still could not credit that she cared for that cad, and he would not believe it until she told him so herself. What the devil was taking so long? His patience at an end, he was about to rap on the door when it suddenly opened.

Rumpole was saying to Damaris, "Well, I believe that concludes my business, at least for this evening. I may have one or two more questions on the morrow, but on the whole I believe you can put this affair behind you."

"Miss Montague will not be charged?" Charles asked worriedly.

"There will be a coroner's inquest, of course, but I should be most surprised if they did not return a verdict of accidental death. Miss Montague, would you be so good as to convey my gratitude to your aunt for her hospitality? I do not wish to disturb her further this evening."

Charles thought it more likely that the investigator did not wish to be pestered further by yet more questions, but he said nothing as Damaris agreed. Emily was dispatched to show Rumpole to the door, and for a few blessed moments, Charles was left alone in the hall with Damaris.

"I should take my leave as well," he told her but remained standing beside her.

"Charles, I . . . I want to apologize. I am so sorry that I did not tell you about that night and about Snelling—"

"Hush," he told her gently. "It would have made matters a great deal easier, but I cannot blame you. There is only one thing that troubles me. When Faustus carried in Snelling's hat, and his body was discovered, you fled to Marling. Did you still intend to fly with him?" Trying to sound unconcerned, he added, "I had thought you no longer cared for him."

Damaris shuddered and Charles immediately put an arm about her shoulders. "Never mind, we need not discuss it if it disturbs you."

Nestled in the comfortable embrace of his arms, her eyes brimming with unshed tears, she whispered, "I do not deserve such kindness, but I cannot allow you to think that I still cared for Marling. I loathed him!"

"Then why did you go to him?" he asked gently, lifting up her chin so he could see her eyes.

"I knew Rumpole would find out I was the one responsible, and I feared they would arrest me for murder."

"Even had they done so, I would have helped you."

She nodded tearfully and explained in a rush, "I know. That is why I had to leave. You have spoken of how much you desire a career in politics, and even Lord Dysart says you have a brilliant future—but if I were labeled a murderess, and your name was linked with mine, it would ruin you. After you had been so kind to me, I could not allow that to happen."

He sighed. "Thank heavens his lordship was there to stop you. Damaris, my darling little idiot, do you not realize that you are far more important to me than a career, or—"

Her arms slipped around his neck as she hugged him warmly. "You called me darling."

"Well, yes. . . ," he replied as her face lifted temptingly to his. His arm tightened about her and he kissed her sweetly. He meant it to be only a brief embrace, but he could no more resist her than he could stop breathing. Charles deepened the kiss, claiming her irrevocably for his own.

When he finally released her, Damaris gazed up at

him. Her tears had dried, but her eyes were shining. "I never knew a kiss could be like that. . . ."

"Like what?" he asked, his voice a trifle breathless.

"So wonderful, so much like . . . like heaven. Oh, Charles!"

Chapter 14

After a quiet breakfast, Juliana returned to her bed-chamber to dress in anticipation of Lord Dysart's call. Both Melody and Damaris had ridden out with Oliver, so she had ample time. From the back of her wardrobe, she removed a walking dress *à la hussar* one of the few she'd brought with her from Morcombe. Of natural cotton, it was a soft tan, and the bodice and long sleeves fit tightly, much like a spencer, and fastened with Brandenburg buttons in the military style. Below the sash of the bodice, the skirt flared and fell in soft folds to the ankles. The collar was rolled, standing a few inches above her shoulders, and with its white lace ruffle, it provided a flattering frame for her slender neck. The dress, created especially for her three years before, had been one of Juliana's favorites. She tried it on, praying that it would still fit.

The buttons were difficult to fasten, and Juliana was thankful when Emily tapped on her door. The slender maid came in, carrying an enormous bouquet of roses that she explained had just been delivered. She handed over the card and, while Juliana read it, buttoned up the back of the walking dress.

"You look lovely, my lady."

Odd to hear herself addressed in such a manner again, Juliana thought. Aloud, she said, "Thank you, but I believe it needs a touch of color." Laying aside the card from Lord Dysart, she removed a tissue-wrapped parcel from the bottom of her wardrobe. "My brother brought me this back from France when he went on the grand tour," she explained as she removed a shawl made of the finest wool with a red floral border and silk fringe. The border was several inches wide and the red and green of the flowers provided the perfect splash of color as she draped it over her arms.

Emily enthusiastically approved. Although she'd thought the dress a shade drab, for she liked the brilliant colors of silks and satins, she had to admit the simple lines of the dress suited Lady Juliana, and told her she looked extremely elegant and fashionable.

When the maid had left, Juliana studied her reflection in the long looking glass once more. She did look fashionable. Unable to sleep, she had risen early and taken pains with her hair. For years she'd worn it done tidily up in a knot, which she'd felt suited her position. But this morning she'd used her combs to pin it back in soft waves and allowed the coppery curls to fall just above the collar.

It was undoubtedly vain of her, but she meant to say farewell to Lord Dysart today, and she did not want his last memory of her to be that of the dowdy companion he was accustomed to seeing. She picked up the card she'd left lying beside the vase of flowers.

The lines scrawled in his own hand were as dark and bold as Dysart himself, and they stirred a yearning in Juliana. *I shall call for you at one. I know the hour is unreasonably early, but I am most anxious to see you.*

Juliana knew the words meant nothing. Lord Dysart was no doubt impatient to put this business behind him and return to his friends in London. She appreciated that his sense of responsibility, and the debt he felt he owed Philip, would not permit him to leave without first making certain that she would not be left to fend for herself. She would have to find a way to persuade him that she no longer needed his assistance and that she could not, under any circumstances, visit his mother. She smiled, imagining how appalled the duchess would be were she to accept Dysart's offer of an extended stay.

As the mantel clock chimed the quarter hour, she walked to the window and looked out at the drive. Although it was near one o'clock, there was no sign yet of Dysart's carriage. She settled in a chair and picked up one of the novels from the lending library. It was a futile effort, as she realized when she read the same sentence over for the third time and it still made little sense. Giving up the pretense, she laid the book aside and stared out the window. At a quarter past one, she wondered what had delayed him. Lord Dysart had always been punctual, and he had written he was anxious to see her. . . .

At half past one, Juliana rose and restlessly paced the room. What could have detained him? Had Rumpole changed his mind? Had there been some unforeseeable problem at Windward? Deeply disappointed, she was on the verge of changing her dress when the sound of carriage wheels drew her to the window once again. She saw Dysart as he descended from the carriage, spoke to his groom, and then strode toward the house. He looked incredibly handsome, she thought wistfully as she donned her straw bonnet. She picked up her reticule and hurried down the flight of stairs that led to the hall.

She saw him speaking to Wilfred as she descended. Then he glanced up and their gazes locked. Ignoring the butler, Lord Dysart crossed the hall and gave Juliana his arm as she came down the last two steps.

"Lady Juliana, my apologies for my tardy arrival. Can you forgive me?"

"After the beautiful flowers you sent, how could I possibly not?"

A thud sounded against the drawing-room door, and a few seconds later Faustus bounded through, followed by Mrs. Throckmorton. She apologized as the dog made straight for Dysart and rubbed against his boots.

"He heard your voice, my lord, and there was no restraining him."

Dysart greeted the older woman, obligingly scratched the sheepdog's ears, then ordered him to sit.

"Amazing," Mrs. Throckmorton said as Faustus instantly obeyed. "But I am forgetting my manners. Would you care for a cup of coffee, or tea, before you go? It would be no trouble."

"Thank you, and I should like to stay, but my mother arrived rather unexpectedly." He turned to Juliana and added, "That is why I was late arriving."

"Your mother," Mrs. Throckmorton uttered. "Gracious, I believe this is the first time the duchess has ever visited Windward. I do hope you will bring her to call."

"She would like very much to make your acquaintance, for I have told her of your kindness to me, but I fear she intends a rather brief visit."

"You must return at once then," Juliana told him, trying not to show her disappointment. "Indeed, there was no reason for you to come yourself. A message would have sufficed."

"There was every reason," he assured her. "The foremost being that Maman is most anxious to meet you."

"Lord Dysart, I cannot—"

"Do not be missish, Lady Juliana," Mrs. Throckmorton advised and gave her a small nudge. "Go along. The duchess is doing you a great honor, and it would be rude to keep her waiting."

Juliana looked helplessly from Dysart to her employer. It appeared she had little choice. Even Wilfred expected her to leave and stood holding open the door.

"You once told me that you thought you would like my mother," the earl reminded her as they walked to his carriage. "Have you changed your opinion?"

She allowed him to assist her into the carriage, and when they were both comfortably seated replied, "I am sure your mother is most charming, but I dislike imposing on her. And there are dozens of things I should be tending to. Mrs. Throckmorton has definitely decided to take the girls to London, and you can have no notion of how much preparation must be done before we can remove." As the carriage rolled forward, she was aware she was blathering and making little sense, but with Dysart sitting opposite her, studying her so intently, she found she could not think clearly.

He leaned forward and took one of her hands in his. "Mrs. Throckmorton is a dear, kind woman, but she is going to have to learn to do without your assistance. I thought we had it settled that when this business with Snelling was done, you would visit Maman."

She withdrew her hand and replied reprovingly, "You said so, my lord, but I never agreed, and I doubt very much if your mother would, either."

He leaned against the cushioned back of the carriage and considered her. "You are very formal today, my dear. Do you think you could manage to refer to me as Val, or Dysart?"

"I . . . I do not think it would be appropriate," she replied, lowering her eyes to avoid his gaze.

"Why? You are the daughter of the sixth Duke of Morcombe, and sister of the Earl of Pymbroke. We are equals, Juliana."

Her name sounded wonderful on his lips, and the warmth of his voice in the intimacy of the carriage did much to weaken her resolve. Only the knowledge that they were on their way to meet his mother gave her the strength to reply firmly, "I am still penniless, my lord, and employed as a companion. I must remember my position even if you choose not to."

"I can see this is going to be more difficult than I had anticipated."

Silence filled the carriage. Uneasily Juliana stole a glance at him. He was watching her, his deep brown eyes full of amusement.

"Did I forget to mention yesterday that I persuaded your cousin to open an account in your name with the Bank of England? He deposited two hundred and fifty pounds to your credit, and will continue to do so every quarter day. Not a fortune, precisely, but—"

"I do not want it," she interrupted stiffly.

"I beg your pardon?"

"I do not wish to seem ungrateful, Lord Dysart, but I do not want his money. Please try to understand—I could not bear to be indebted to Lucian. I want nothing from him, my lord, not his money, not his kinship. I would rather starve first."

"Juliana, do not be foolish. This money belonged to your father and your grandfather. You are entitled to it, and if Lucian had been any decent sort of man, he would have set up an allowance for you long since." In truth, her cousin had refused to grant her so much as a sixpence, and Dysart himself had created the account, with strict instructions that Lady Juliana was not to know the source of her funds. The money meant little to him. He could well afford to be generous, and he would have given it to her outright, except he knew she would never accept it. He had not wanted her to feel dependent on anyone, but he had not counted on her stubborn pride.

As they neared the house, Dysart rapped sharply on the

roof of the carriage, then ordered Toby to pull to the side of the road.

"What are you doing?" Juliana asked a trifle nervously.

"I believe there are a few matters we must settle before you meet my mother, and I prefer to discuss them in private. Therefore I suggest a walk. You do not have any objections to walking with me, I hope?"

Juliana did, but feeling now was not the time to voice her protests, she answered meekly, "No, my lord."

When the carriage rolled to a halt, Dysart climbed down, lowered the steps, then assisted Juliana to alight. He ordered Toby to drive on to the house. "We shall walk from here."

They were not far from the curving drive and the wrought iron gates that led to Windward. The day was sunny but not overly warm, and Dysart offered his arm. When Juliana reluctantly laid her hand upon his sleeve, he strolled slowly forward, saying, "Now, my lady, I have tried to bide my time. I have tried to respect your notions of propriety, and to wait until you felt reasonably comfortable with me, but I can see stronger measures are called for. My mother will likely think me run mad if we arrive at the house and you continue to address me so primly as 'my lord.'"

"She would doubtless be very much shocked if I did otherwise," Juliana protested.

"Allow me to know my mother better than you," Dysart answered. They were now hidden by the hedgerows just before the gate, and the road was empty of carriages or persons. He turned her gently to face him. "Look at me, Juliana," he ordered when she kept her gaze down.

"My lord, I am sure this is most improper—"

Placing his hand beneath her chin, he forced her head

up. "Val. 'Tis a very simple name and takes little breath to utter. Try it, my dear."

"Val," she murmured, and felt thankful it was a short name, for she suddenly found it most difficult to speak.

"Very good. It will come easier with time," he approved, gazing down into her turquoise eyes. Today they were a deep blue, with only a hint of green. A pale flush suffused her cheeks, and her lips . . . her enticing lips were parted slightly. "You are not nervous of me?"

"No. . . ."

"Good," he whispered, and somehow his hands slipped around her waist, drawing her closer. She was so slender, her waist so tiny he could easily span it with his hands. He fought his desire to crush her close to him and urged, "Say it again."

"Val . . . we must not . . . ohh!"

As her lips had opened to pronounce his name, he had captured them with his own, his mouth savoring the delicious sweetness of her as he had longed to do since that first morning he'd seen her. He felt her hands move to his shoulders, then creep about his neck as his own hands tightened around her.

He deepened the kiss for an all too brief moment, then lifted his head. Her eyes were closed, the long lashes lying sweetly against her face. He released her slightly, then waited until she gazed up at him. Her expression was one of wonderment and yearning, and a thrill of exaltation shot through him. If he were a few years younger, he would have scaled the stone walls of Windward and shouted his jubilation from the roof.

Controlling himself with an effort, he smiled down at her. "Much better, my dear. Now promise me you will be sensible and accept this stipend from your cousin. It will allow you to be sufficiently independent that you will not have to be at Miss Montague's beck and call."

Evading a direct answer, she replied, "I would far rather answer to Damaris than to my cousin."

"It is not necessary that you do either. Accept the allowance he is willing to provide you, my dear. It does not mean that you ever have to see or acknowledge him. Indeed, I believe it advisable that you have nothing at all to do with your cousin."

"I do not intend to, but I am curious—how did you convince Lucian to withdraw the charges against me?"

Dysart grinned. "You have Charles to thank, at least in part. He'd told me that he suspected your cousin was involved in smuggling, using the cove at Morcombe to move the goods in and out. I suspect it is why he stays so close to home."

"And you confronted him? Oh, Val, I wish you had not. Lucian is so vindictive—he will try to find a way to make you suffer for your interference."

"I doubt it. My darling, your cousin is not quite the ogre you think him. He was not responsible for half the incidents laid at his door, but he has allowed people to think he was because it suited him to be feared. He habitually wears black just to enhance the image."

She shook her head. "He burned the letters I wrote, and he fabricated the charges against me."

"He did, but aside from his smuggling, that is about the extent of his activities. He caved in quickly enough when I threatened to have him arrested. I also made certain he knew I had written statements regarding his smuggling operation that would be turned over to the authorities should anything happen to me. After that, it was a simple matter to convince him to withdraw the charges against you."

"I still cannot believe it," she murmured. "When I saw him come in the door with you, I nearly fainted."

Dysart kissed the tip of her nose. "Put him from your mind, darling. I doubt he will ever trouble you again. But

. . . he is a most unsavory fellow, and I should not be at all surprised if he brings disgrace to your family. . . . I, uh, I think it might even be wise if you considered changing your name."

"Continue to use Spencer, do you mean? I had thought of it, but—"

"Not Spencer," he interrupted, his arms tightening around her once again. Could she feel the way his heart was racing? "I had in mind something more like Kinborough. . . . Juliana, my darling, in my own clumsy fashion, I am trying to ask you to be my wife."

"You cannot be serious," she said and tried to step back from his embrace.

He held her prisoner within his arms. "I have never been more serious in my life."

For a brief second hope flared, then died as suddenly, leaving an aching void. She looked away so he could not see the heartache in her eyes. "You are very kind, but even Philip would not expect you to make such a sacrifice."

He groaned but spoke with infinite patience, "Your brother has nothing to do with this. I was extremely fond of Philip, but I am asking you to be my wife because it is what I wish. Juliana, do you recall that evening when I asked what you would do if Lucian appeared?"

When she nodded, he continued, "I knew then I was in love with you. The idea of never seeing you again . . . it was unthinkable. I knew then that I could not bear to live without you, darling. Juliana?"

Tears brimming her lashes, she hid her face against his shoulder. "Even if that were true, we could not . . . your family . . . a dreadful misalliance."

The words were muffled but he caught the intent clearly enough. At least it was her sense of propriety, and not a rejection of him, that fueled her resistance. The edge of her bonnet poked against his cheek. Releasing her for a second, he reached up and quickly undid the ribbons tied beneath her chin.

As he lifted the hat free, he told her, "As I recall, it was a straw bonnet that provided our first introduction. How appropriate that another should seal our betrothal."

"My lord! Val, you must not—"

But he had cast the hat over the hedgerow and in the next instant gathered her in his arms and kissed her thoroughly until she was too breathless and too stunned to protest further.

"You will make an excellent countess," he murmured when he finally lifted his head. "As for my family, I will have you know that my mother traveled here at great speed and with tremendous discomfort only to ensure that I did not leave Windward without proposing to you."

She stared up at him, wanting to believe but afraid to.

"It's perfectly true," he assured her. "She told me it was obvious from my letter that I was in love with you. She just was not certain that I knew it. Of course I do—as I told you, I have known it for quite some time."

"But you never said. . . . you never did anything to indicate—"

"How could I?" he asked reasonably but could not refrain from kissing the tip of her nose. "My love is a perfect lady who refused to dance with me or to drive with me . . ." He punctuated his words with feather-light kisses on both her brows. "How could I say a word until she was in a position, finally, to accept my offer?" He kissed her mouth then, a long, lingering caress that stilled whatever doubts she might have had.

When he finally released her, he gazed adoringly down at her. "Does this lack of resistance mean that you accept my offer?"

Blushing furiously, she murmured, "If you are certain your mother will not object. . . ."

"Did I not tell you she was anxious for grandchildren? She is waiting to welcome you, and we should go . . . but perhaps a few more moments," he whispered as he leaned forward to kiss her once again.

Inside the house known as Windward, the Duchess of Pymbroke waited impatiently for her son to arrive. When a quarter hour had passed, she spoke to Charles. "What can be keeping them? Toby said he set them down near the gate, and that was nearly half an hour past. Do you think Lady Juliana has refused him? Charles, I could not bear it. I believe it would break his heart. If you had seen the letter he wrote me—"

"I think it highly unlikely she would refuse him. Trust me, Your Grace, she is equally in love."

"Then perhaps something has happened, an accident or—Charles, would you walk down the drive and see?"

Having a very good idea of what was detaining his lordship, Charles nevertheless agreed. He took his time, strolling leisurely down the drive. It was a beautiful day, and if he'd had Damaris with him, he, too, would dally. But it was unkind to keep the duchess waiting.

As he drew near the gate, a straw bonnet sailed over the hedgerows. Curious, he crossed the sweep of lawn and picked it up. A very charming straw hat, and if he was not mistaken, it belonged to Lady Juliana. He laughed aloud. Charles had heard of young ladies setting their caps for gentlemen, but this was absurd.

Then he heard Dysart's low voice, and the soft responsive laughter of a lady. He peered around the corner of the gate and smiled. Apparently Lord Dysart had settled matters to his satisfaction. Only a cad would interrupt such a moment.

Whistling softly, Charles made his way back up the drive to tell the duchess her son would be delayed yet a few more moments. He thought he might take her the hat.